The Rhad were a melancholy race, and Kier felt the weight of the dour centuries in his heart, so it jarred him to hear Marlana's laughter.

"Oh you out-worlders," she said. "What an ancient breed you are! Glamiss used to say, 'The Rhad see doom beyond every hill.' Is it because you live so far away, Rebel? Out on the edge of the sky where there are no stars to see in the night? Where is your ambition, you brave captain? I'm offering you the Inner Worlds if you are man enough to take them!"

"You mean treacherous enough," Kier replied.

ROBERT CHAM GILMAN

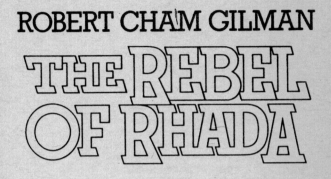

THE REBEL OF RHADA

ACE SCIENCE FICTION BOOKS
NEW YORK

THE REBEL OF RHADA

An Ace Science Fiction Book/published by arrangement with
the author

PRINTING HISTORY
Harcourt, Brace & World edition published 1968
Ace Science Fiction edition/January 1986

ISBN: 0-441-71068-9

Ace Science Fiction Books are published by
The Berkley Publishing Group,
200 Madison Avenue, New York, New York 10016.
PRINTED IN THE UNITED STATES OF AMERICA

For Ann and Trey, who have been Sharane and John Carter

Chapter One

—dielectric interphasers stabilize primary spatiotem-poral valences, making access to the engine cores unnecessary—and extremely hazardous. Core serv-icing will be performed only *by qualified personnel in Imperial Naval Starship Facilities (Class A7 or above). However, since the estimated service life of the stellar drive unit has been computed to be 10^6 Earth Standard Years, it is extremely unlikely—*

—speed of star class vessels may be varied from 0 kps (hovering atmospheric flight) to 10^9 kps (inter-system transit). Crew training has been simplified to an extreme—

> Golden Age fragments found
> at Station One, Astraris

> 'Ware the spirit of sin that lives within
> The strength of the god that holds the rod
> In the ship that can fly
> To the end of the sky
> Never seek WHY or you will DIE!

> Chant from the *Book of Warls,*
> Interregnal period

1

*Though our knowledge is faulty and our resources
meager, yet, brothers, the starships live and they are
our trust. What the ignorant call sin men once called
science, and we will recover it one day for all mankind.*

> Attributed to Emeric of Rhada,
> Grand Master of Navigators,
> early Second Stellar Empire

THE starship was ancient: no one knew how ancient,
yet the mysterious force magically generated within
the core drove it across the starry darkness with immense speed.

The interior of the great vessel was close and smoky,
for the only light came from gymballed lamps and
torches. These were kept low, but they still slowly
fouled the air. Once there had been light without fire
in the thousand-meter-long hulls, but the life-support
systems—which were not one with the magical force
that drove the ships—had failed time out of mind.
Deep in the hull, near the keel, the chambers housing
the inoperative systems were stables for the muttering
war mares.

These animals were accustomed to star travel, and
the small detachment of Rhad warmen aboard tended
them well. But they complained and were restless in
their confinement.

Forward, in that part of the starship forbidden to
any but consecrated Navigators, two novices and the
priest chanted the position and queried the ship's com-
puters. This was ritual. At intervals of six Standard
Hours, each member of the Order of Navigators, if
he was in space, must sing his calculations. At this
moment, across the galaxy, separated by parsecs of
emptiness, perhaps a thousand Navigators, all who

were traveling at a given moment in time, were busy with positions and agreements.

The starship fled through a strange environment that was space become fluid time. Though the men who controlled its movements did so by rote, not understanding what they did or why, the vessel moved at many times the speed of light, and this caused strange effects: the stars ahead clustered in a pulsing violet ellipsoid. Those behind were deep red. This was The Mystery of the Red Shift. Since the founding of the Order, Navigators had composed canticles and convened synods to ponder this miracle. But no learned priest had ever explained it.

On the control deck, position was sung to completion and compared with the archaically phrased information given by the ship. The Navigators made the sign of the Star in thanksgiving for an agreement with the ship, and the ritual came to an end. The watch could now change hands.

The priest Kalin surrendered his place to Brother John, the senior of the two novices, and with a last glimpse at the violet stars ahead and the red stars astern, left the control deck.

The priest was a young man, his figure running a little to plumpness under his robes and mail; but his face had the clear, rather melancholy features of the noble house of Rhad, for he was blood cousin as well as bond-priest and Navigator to Kier, the warleader of Rhada.

He walked familiarly through the maze of companionways toward the living spaces of the ship. Occasionally, his weapons would strike the walls, and they would ring like bells, for they were fashioned of god-metal. It was his right as a member of the ruling family of the Rhadan worlds. Other men might carry implements of base iron, but not the Rhad.

Kalin was thinking of the starship's destination—
Earth, and the imperial city of Nyor. Though Kalin
was noble, he had never seen the fabled city between
the two rivers on the brow of Tel-Manhat. The priest's
youth had been spent on Astraris and his young man-
hood on Algol Two, in the Theocracy, where the Navigators' cloister had stood for a thousand years.

His duties after ordination had taken him to a half
dozen of the Rim worlds, but he had never seen the
Empire's Inner Marches. He looked forward to Earth
with excitement.

He considered himself favored to have been bonded
to his cousin Kier. Navigators had no nationality, of
course. This was the will of God. But even the beatified Emeric had never forgotten that he was once a
noble Rhad.

Kalin, young as he was, had already served rulers
whose service he was pleased to leave. To be bonded
to his cousin Kier of Rhada was a far greater piece
of luck than he had dared to wish for. Yet here he
was, Navigator in command of a Rhadan starship, and
best of all, headed for Imperial Earth, where his cousin
had been summoned by no less a personage than Torquas Primus, Galacton, King of the Universe, Protector of the Faith, Defender of the Inner and Outer
Marches, Commander of the Starfleets, and who could
remember what other magnificent titles.

As he drew near the living spaces now, he encountered groups of warmen lounging, gaming, or
caring for their weapons. And as he passed, they stood
to salute him—not with the sign of the Star due a
priest-Navigator, but with the military salute given
only to members of the ruling house of Rhada.

He should have reproached them for lack of piety,

but he could not resist the urge to be pleased at their recognition of his family rank. He sighed and told himself that he would have to allot himself a proper penance for his pride—five hundred logarithms (he hated reciting logarithms) or perhaps fifty Ave Stellas.

In the starkly bare and cavernous compartment near the center of the ship, Kier, warleader of Rhada, was also thinking of Imperial Earth, Torquas Primus, and pride.

The warleader was a young man, too, hardly months older than his cousin the priest-Navigator, but he seemed older.

He was tall, slender, with the muscular figure of a man trained from infancy for war. His hair was dark and cropped to be worn beneath a helmet. His polished mail gleamed in the lamplight, and his sword and weapons, though plain, were well cared for. Only the fur edging on his cape marked his rank, for he was a son of Aaron the Devil, an austere man who taught his son that wealth was land and fighting men, not fine harness.

Kier had spent his cadetship in the service of Willim of Astraris, a Rhad, but no pamperer of royal cubs for all of that. A second cousin of old Aaron, Willim held Astraris and Gonlan, the two outer worlds of the Rhadan Palatinate. Under his guidance, young Kier had learned to read and write, to study some history and the old legends from his own warlock, and to fight.

He had learned first to handle his weapons and a war horse, then to lead small formations of warmen, and finally—when Willim thought proper—to lead armies as large as five and six thousand men. When all this was done, Kier's education was considered complete, and he was returned to his father's court. And none too soon, for Aaron, spent with the constant warfare of the Rim worlds, died shortly thereafter and left the kingship of the Palatinate to Kier.

The Palatinate was a turbulent confederation of ten planets circling four Rim stars. Kier spent his first years of kingship fighting rebellious nobles, then hopeful invaders from the Inner Marches, and finally the enemies of Glamiss of Vyka, the man who became the first to hold the title of Galacton.

Interspersed with these legitimate battles, Kier fought enough skirmishes with the authorities of the Empire over taxes and land rights to earn the nickname of Rebel.

Yet the Rhadans were generally loyal to the Second Empire; indeed they had helped to establish it. Kier had led a division of mixed Rhadans and Astrari in Glamiss's army at the Battle of Karma, and he had stood at the Emperor's right hand when Casso the Pretender met the ax.

At twenty-three, Kier had been leader of his people for five years. There were eighteen million Rhadans thinly holding their ten worlds. Of necessity life was hard in the Palatinate, and all the men (and most of the women, too) were warriors. The young ruler must therefore be severe, and so he was by heredity and training. But in the company of friends, the forbidding manner of the professional warman vanished, to be replaced by a warm and generous charm. His warmen, accustomed to sharing their hardships with him, were loyal. It was they who called him The Rebel, because though he served the House of Vyka as all the star kings were required to do, he would defy all the Empire to protect his own.

In spite of this, Kier considered himself a loyal captain of the Vykan Emperors.

At this moment, however, his loyalty seemed in doubt. The great noble whom the priest Kalin thought of as Torquas Primus, Galacton, King of the Universe, and so on, was, in fact, a twelve-year-old boy surrounded by plunderers. He was a sprig of the old oak, Glamiss the Magnificent, but showed no promise of growing into half the man his father had been—or, for that matter, of growing up at all.

In the three years since the Emperor Glamiss's death in some out-world brawl, the court favorites and the Empress-Consort, wife of the boy ruler, had fastened onto him. They seemed set on milking the vassal worlds of everything of value, and the Rim worlds seethed with revolt.

It seemed to Kier that Imperial oppression and greed would soon, if allowed to continue, destroy Glamiss's work and tumble the Second Stellar Empire into a black age more terrible than the unnumbered centuries that had followed the collapse of the First.

The Empress-Consort Marlana and her warleader, Landro, had come to know Kier's opinions, it seemed.

Kier sat on the high seat and stared in moody silence at the shadowy hall hung with ornamental war gear. He was alone in the great compartment except for Gret, the creature who had been his father's fool.

Gret was a Vulk, a member of the only other intelligent race men had ever found in all the vast reaches of space. Humanoid, small of stature, with an eyeless face and an immense head, he resembled nothing in all the experience of men but what he was—a Vulk.

Vulks did not *see* or *hear* as men did. They reacted

to things and beings around them in some impossible Vulk way, as though they responded to some aura or essence that stimulated the very special Vulk mind.

A Vulk might "see" a beautiful woman and know her ugly or a fierce war horse and know him gentle under his fear. They could turn their blind faces to complicated masses of wreckage, machinery of the Golden Age, and divine the purpose for which the machines were built. Warlocks said that with their powers they could rule the galaxy. But they were a race without ambition, as humans know ambition. And to their cost they were a race without violence. The savage human tides that surged through space during the Black Age and in the time of the Interregnal Wars had exterminated them in hundreds of thousands.

The mobs who followed the armies burning witches and warlocks and sometimes priests and rulers also butchered Vulks wherever they could be found. By the time of the Vykan Reconquest, the Vulk colonies that had spread throughout the galaxy under the protection of the Golden Age emperors were no more.

The few aliens who survived the pogroms found refuge in the courts of the out-land rulers of the Rim worlds, who valued them for their strange ways and skills.

Gret could sing with the voice of an angel, human melodies and mystically beautiful Vulk laments. He could recite all the ancient battles and guest songs, play musical instruments, and tell many strange stories of worlds no man ever knew. And it had always seemed to Kier that Gret owned a wisdom that was more than human, though it took peculiar and oddly disturbing forms.

The young warman turned now in his seat to look at his companion, who sat on the deck at his feet, toying with a stringed instrument.

"Gret," he said quietly, "do Vulks die?" He was thinking that he could not remember a time when Gret was not near, and in his father's time, too, it had been so.

The Vulk stirred. "You know that they do, King." The eyeless, pale face glistened in the lamplight. "You have seen them dead in plenty."

"I have seen them killed," Kier said. "I asked you if Vulks died."

"Everything under the stars, or among them, dies, King. Sometime," the Vulk said with a ghostly smile. "We need never ask *if*—only when, King."

The young star king smiled back at the Vulk, recognizing the warning and the personal love that prompted it. That was the way of it. No Vulk ever answered a question directly.

But one thing was certain. Kier had never seen one of Gret's kind dead of natural causes. He could not imagine how old Gret was. He had been Aaron's fool, and before that Aaron's father's fool. The ignorant whispered that Vulks lived forever.

"Human beings die," Gret said, plucking a string on his instrument. "Even star kings."

Kier's smile slowly faded. He did not need warnings to know his danger. In times past an Imperial summons might have meant a coming war, a royal commission.

But things were no longer as they had been when Glamiss ruled. Torquas commanded him to Earth "with only those of your household needful to your comfort." In other words, without his personal troops.

Caught in a dilemma between loyalty and common sense, Kier had compromised by bringing only Gret and his personal warlock, Cavour, and a single squadron of picked warmen under command of his lieuten-ant-general, Nevus. Politics was the business of star kings, and politics in the second decade of the Second Stellar Empire consisted largely of staying alive.

Kier listened to the humming of the ship. His cousin Kalin was due with a position report soon. Kier, ex-perienced in star travel, estimated that they were now less than six Earth Standard Hours from Nyor.

Once Cavour had attempted to determine by cal-culation the exact speed of the fifteen starships under Rhadan control. This was perilous research, for it infringed on the Holy Mysteries. A generation earlier, the inquisitors of the Order of Navigators had ordered warlocks burned for less. But Cavour was a free spirit, and he could not rest until he had attempted the puzzle. He had studied the fragments found at Station One on Astraris (the First Empire ruins there had once been an A8 facility, whatever *that* was), and after days of laborious computations he had offered Kier the in-credible figure of two hundred thousand kilometers per hour. This would have been the equivalent of circumnavigating Rhada eight times in sixty minutes. The Astrari warlocks had laughed poor Cavour out of their workshops, pointing out that since a starship made the voyage from Rhada and the Rim worlds to Earth in slightly more than forty-nine hours, Cavour's calculations would mean that the galaxy must be twelve *million*, eight hundred *thousand* kilometers in diam-eter. This immense figure was so patently absurd that even Cavour was shaken. He reluctantly abandoned his hypothesis and concluded that whatever meaning there was in the Golden Age fragments that turned up from time to time on Astraris, his own mathematics had somewhere gone badly astray.

* * *

Kier stood and began to pace restlessly about the compartment. Above his head, a great blank screen was dimly visible. The legends said that in the Golden Age such screens, which were everywhere in the starships, had shown the things that were happening outside the vessels. How such a thing might be, Kier did not know, but he believed it because he knew that the men of the First Empire had been workers of miracles. Still, sin had destroyed them, bringing the darkness of the Interregnal Wars, leaving their great works everywhere shattered.

The screens—like the globes in the overheads, like the machines that freshened the air in the ships, like thousands of other artifacts whose purpose the men of this age could scarcely fathom—had not worked for thousands of years. Light came from fire, not mysterious globes. And one could see *outside* only from the forbidden chambers of the starship, places where an unconsecrated man, even a star king, could not go. Kier had never seen the stars from space. Regretfully, he knew that he never would. Only Kalin and his kind could do that.

"Gret," he said impatiently. "Give us a song." He went back to his seat and waited to be obeyed.

"What will you hear, King?"

"Sense me. You will know." A Vulk always knew what one wanted—sometimes better than one knew oneself.

Gret cradled his instrument and leaned his narrow back against the young star king's chair. "Hear me, then."

He struck a chord with his long, delicate fingers and then began to sing.

"'If thou be'st born to strange sights,
    Things invisible to see,
Ride ten thousand days and nights,
    Till Age snow white hairs on thee;
Thou, when thou return'st, wilt tell me
All strange wonders that befell thee,
        And swear
        No where
Lives a woman true and fair.'"

He struck a last note, and it hung melodically in the humming air. Then silence fell.

Presently, Kier said, "Was I thinking of the Empress-Consort, then?"

Gret smiled slowly. "You were not."

"Then?"

"Shall I guess, King? Is it Earth we are going to?"

Kier stared at the Vulk. Could one love such a baffling and contentious creature?

"Tell me," he commanded.

"The King does not know his own mind?"

"I said, 'Tell me,'" Kier said sternly.

"You were remembering a reedy girl who loved you on Karma. A great personage. The daughter of a mighty king." The Vulk strummed another chord and let it die away.

"Ariane."

"The very same," Gret said.

Kier laughed. The daughter of Glamiss had been thirteen years old the year the Battle of Karma was fought and even then betrothed to the star king of Fomalhaut, a lord of the Inner Marches, old and rich in men and worlds.

But no news of an Imperial marriage had reached the Rim worlds. Marlana, the Empress-Consort,

wanted no Princess Royal with the resources of twenty
worlds at her back.

Where was Ariane now, Kier wondered. She would
be seventeen—no, almost nineteen now.

"The song," the warleader said. "I don't know it."

"It was written by a man of your own race, King."

"A Rhadan?"

"Oh, no. There were no men on Rhada in this poet's
time. Would you believe me if I told you he lived
eleven thousand years ago?"

Kier smiled and shook his head. Vulks, he thought
tolerantly. They spoke in parables and riddles. Everyone knew the first men were created by God 6,606
years before the founding of the First Stellar Empire.

"A man of the Golden Age, then?"

The Vulk said, "One who lived before the Golden
Age, before the first human being left the Earth. His
name was Donne."

"And how do you know that, Gret?"

The Vulk played a delicate tune on a single string.
"What is good is remembered, King."

Kier would have liked to hear more of this poet
who Gret claimed lived so long ago, but at this moment his cousin, the Navigator Kalin, entered and
saluted him.

"We will make our planetfall in five hours, cousin,"
the Navigator said.

Kier made the sign of the Star and murmured, as
required, "God be praised."

"Blessed be the name of God," Kalin responded.
Then he smiled at the warleader. Kalin thoroughly
approved of Kier. He was courageous, properly noble,
and devout in his observances. A fit descendant of
the finest of the Rhad, the beatified Emeric.

Kalin, who was a generous-minded and rather simple young man, knew himself to be a good priest-Navigator, though, he often told himself regretfully, not destined to be a great one. The Rhad family had produced one outstanding religious only, and this was Emeric, who had risen to the rank of Grand Master of Navigators a generation ago to lead the Order into a new age of enlightenment. Probably Emeric, Kalin thought, would approve of the second star king of Rhada, too.

Emeric had believed, as had Glamiss the Magnificent, that men should recover all that they had lost in the Black Age. He had even dared to suggest that the time might come when a united mankind might have to face unspecified dangers from outside the galaxy, for he believed that the men of the First Stellar Empire had established, and then lost contact with, colonies in the Lesser Magellanic Cloud. Such a thing seemed inconceivable to Kalin. But if Emeric had believed it, then it was not to be thought impossible.

"Gret was telling me," Kier said to his cousin, "of a singer of songs who lived—how long ago, Gret?"

"Eleven thousand years, King. Give or take a century or two," the Vulk said.

Kalin frowned at the Vulk. The dogma stated very clearly that life began 6,606 years before the founding of the Empire. Gret should not tell such fairy stories. They were dangerously near to heresy, though there were warlocks nowadays who disputed the dogma. It was all confusing to Kalin, who had taken only the barest requirements in theology, preferring to specialize in studies more relevant to his primary duty as Spiritual and Temporal Guide of Starships.

"Well, eleven thousand or not, Gret, it was a fine

song. You shall play it tonight at dinner for our Navigator and make his shaky theology totter. But not this moment." He addressed himself to his cousin and said, "Send an orderly to collect Cavour and Nevus. If we are to reach Nyor in five hours, we have plans to make."

"Will there be ceremonies, Kier?" Kalin asked. "I have brought my finest robe and cowl. I thought it wise."

Kier put an arm across his cousin's shoulders. "I hope you have brought your largest war horse and sharpest weapons. There may be ceremonies of a sort we don't anticipate."

The Navigator looked perplexed. "Are we in danger?"

"I hope not, Kalin," Kier said.

"We are, though. You think so."

Kier half smiled. "It is the way of things in this time, cousin."

"But we have warmen," Kalin said, adjusting to the idea of danger.

"Only enough to hold the starship if we are attacked. More would have looked like rebellion."

"But Kier—on *Earth?* Why would anyone trouble us? Isn't this a state visit—?" He broke off, feeling frustratingly naive and innocent. He looked at his warrior cousin for explanation. "I mean, Kier, I know things have changed since The Magnifico's time, but the Imperials would never dare—" He stopped, suddenly aware that he was in no way sure what, exactly, the Imperials would dare, or even why.

"Find me Cavour and Nevus," Kier said. "Then join us here. I want you to hear what is said. A holy Navigator you may be, but you're a Rhad, too. If there is trouble, I want you to know what to do."

"As you command, King," Kalin said with sudden, grave formality.

Gret's eyeless face grew somber as the Navigator went. He began to play on the strings, making mournful and non-human melodies that only brushed the senses.

"To be so young," he said murmuringly, "to be so innocent and to go into such danger. It is sad, King."

Kier's eyes narrowed. "What danger, Gret?"

"We know. Both of us know." The music wove a strange and age-old pattern in the way of Vulk laments. "Sarissa," the fool said. The sibilant name seemed to mingle with the dirge.

Kier laid a hand across the strings and stopped the music in midflight. "What do you know about Sarissa, Gret?"

The Vulk shrugged, a human gesture Kier would understand. But what did the motion mean to Gret, Kier wondered.

"I know what there is to know," the Vulk said. "I know that the star kings of the Rim worlds gather there. There is talk of rebellion and war against the Empire."

"The redress of grievances, Gret," Kier said in a hard voice.

The Vulk shook his head in denial. "Rebellion, King. And we Vulks remember the Black Age, the time of darkness, the centuries of war and death between the Empires." He struck a deep, resonant note. "Rebellion, King. Your father would weep."

"How do you know of this?" Kier spoke harshly.

"Vulks know. And this, too, I know—that you are undecided and that you will try to buy relief from Torquas for Rhada with a renewed pledge of loyalty."

"Landro, Marlana, and the Imperials are bleeding

us white, Gret. Military service is all the Rhad have
to offer—and it was always enough in Glamiss's time.
Now they demand goods and money we do not have.
I have complained so that I've been summoned to
answer for it." Kier stood and held his sheathed sword
in both clenched fists. "I love the Empire, Gret, as
my father before me loved it. But I am a Rhad of
Rhada—"

"The star king is father to his people," Gret said
with Vulk formality.

"Will Marlana accept my terms?" There was no
more talk of Torquas. Both Vulk and man knew where
the power lay.

"This I do not know, King. But you are putting
yourself into great danger to make terms without armed
men in plenty behind you."

"I know they call me The Rebel," the young star
king said. "But I cannot call on The Magnifico's son
with an army. On Karma the Emperor was more than
my general; he was like a father." He drew the great
sword halfway from its sheath and looked at the glistening blue god-metal of the blade. "I had this from
his own hand, Gret." Gently, he sheathed the blade.
"No, I had no choice. I had to come alone."

The Vulk bowed his head and struck the strings.
He did not say that Kier was not alone and that, if he
was taken, all aboard this starship would die. That
was the way of things in this time. Everyone aboard
this starship belonged to the star king. It was fitting.

He struck the strings again. "When the history of
the Rhad is written, King," he said, "and when all
the battles are songs"—he lifted his blind face to the
young man and smiled—"men will search time, from
the age of cybs and demons to the hour we call now.
And you will be remembered as the greatest of all the

Rhad. Greater than Aaron the Devil, greater even than the holy Emeric. If—" He paused and suddenly drew a flurry of savage and martial sounds from the delicate heart of the lyre. "If you are alive tomorrow, King."

Chapter Two

—biochemical interactions to be kept rigidly within the prescribed parameters because, without exact control, the DNA molecules will be unstable and the life sequence will fail to become self-sustaining.

Extremely high-power requirements demand that any ex—

Golden Age fragment found
at Sardis, Sarissa

Blood of the child, salts of the ground
Give pain with the power and listen for sound
Pray now to sin
To let life begin
A heartbeat inside
Or the old ones have lied.

From the *Book of Warls*,
Interregnal period

THE leather-armored patrolmen walked in pairs in this quarter of the city; the light of their poled lantern cast a yellow light on the damp stone of the walls, so that they went in a pool of brightness that marred the gloom of Sarissa's perpetual dusk.

In the rotting buildings, the poor of Sardis lived in squalor. A few of the more enterprising entertained the warmen on leave who were Sarissa's only visitors, and as the patrolmen went, they could hear the sounds of shrill laughter, strains of rasping music, and the occasional cry of alarm of some drugged or drunken warman awakened to his peril too late.

The patrolmen paid no attention to these sounds of lawlessness. They were accustomed to them, and they had no desire to remain near the house of the warlock on the Street of Night.

The warlock's name was Kelber, and it was known that he lived under the protection of the new warleader of Sarissa, Tallan. But even without the warleader's contemptuous protection, no patrolman would have disturbed the old warlock at his mysterious, sinful work. No Sarissan passed the crumbling stone house on the Street of Night without a thrill of superstitious horror and the sign of the Star in the air to ward off the warlock's familiar devils.

So the patrolmen, with unknowing irony, called the *All's Well* and passed swiftly by. And within the house the cry went unheard, for the walls were meters thick. For a thousand years no house had been built on Sarissa that was not a fortress. The planet had a dark and bloody history, with a succession of savage kings and warleaders of which Tallan, called The Unknown because no man knew from whence he came, was only the most recent.

The warlock's workshop lay at the back of the stronghold, near a warren of storerooms that had once held weapons and food. The walls were crusted with white salts, for the house backed against the vast desolation of the Great Terminator Marsh, a bog that covered most of the land area of the planet's single continent.

Few Sarissans realized the extent of this immense marsh. Indeed, few Sarissans knew that their world was a sphere, an astronomical anomaly: the single planet of a dull red star.

There was no sky on Sarissa. The cloud layer lay at ten thousand meters. In three thousand years, since the planet was first occupied by men, the clouds had never parted.

The oxygen content of the air was low, and Sarissa had bred a brutish race of savage, slow-witted men from the original colonists who had come here, for God knew what reason, in the last years of the Golden Age.

Within the old warlock's laboratory, the walls were damp and the air cold. Strange, ancient machines crowded the floor. Books and fragments of old manuscripts were piled on tables and benches. Stuffed creatures from half a dozen worlds hung grotesquely from the vaulted ceiling. The room had a smell of age and decay.

It could have been the workshop of any witch or warlock anywhere in the Empire, except that it was not lit with lamps or torches but by electricity.

Heavy cables, the insulation checked and worn, snaked about the floor, eventually to vanish into one of the storerooms. This chamber was filled, from wall to wall and floor to ceiling, with an astonishing collection of storage cells, batteries of every shape and size, scavenged by Kelber from half a hundred ancient mounds and ruins. The battered machines powered by this tangle of cables and batteries all carried the ancient Star blazon of the legendary First Stellar Empire.

Magical devices, they were, built by the god-men of the Golden Age.

Even with Tallan's tolerance, the patrolmen would not have spared this room or its contents had they the courage to investigate it. In dread and panic, they would have put the old man to the sword and the house to the torch. Sin, the terrible power of darkness that had destroyed the Golden Age, was everywhere. But no patrolman had troubled Kelber since the new star king began to rule; besides, the old warlock was failing and growing feeble and half mad with age and disappointment.

He crouched over a worktable now, consulting an ancient book, shaking his head and talking to himself. He limped from the book to one of the machines and made an adjustment with gnarled, arthritic hands.

He was gray-bearded and dirty. He could not remember when he had last eaten, nor did he care.

He wormed his way through the clutter to a half-formed, almost human thing sprouting wires and tubes that lay on a metal frame in the center of the room.

He turned an hourglass and mended a broken connection, chittering and mumbling to himself. When he had done, he shuffled to a control panel and closed a switch, and immediately some of the ancient machines began to hum and the air filled with an acrid smell of burning.

The man-thing on the rack twitched and shuddered and then lay still, its flesh bubbling where the wires entered.

The warlock dashed the hourglass against the wall in a fury. He trembled with demented anger, bobbing up and down, trying to *remember,* muttering old chants from the *Book of Warls,* the black bible of warlocks. But it was useless, *useless*. Why couldn't he *remem-*

ber? How had he grown so old, so *forgetful*—?

From the dark doorway came the sound of laughter, contemptuous and cold. "Another failure, Grandfather."

The old man returned to his desk and began rooting like an animal in the piled confusion of papers.

"Back to the *Warls,* is it?" The speaker stepped into the light. He was a large man, immensely strong, proportioned with a powerful grace that no Sarissan could hope to match. He wore a dark cloak and cowl.

The warlock frowned and said crossly, "Power is what I need. Power. I used it and it is gone! How did the ancients do it, *how?* Where did the new life in the batteries come from? Where did they find it?"

"Try chanting, Grandfather," the cloaked man said ironically, turning back his cowl.

His face was inhumanly handsome, lofty, noble. Only the old warlock knew that it was the face of an actor of the Golden Age, a man four thousand years dead, and the warlock had forgotten.

"I did it once," the old man said with the stubborn anger of age.

"A miracle," the large man said with sarcastic piety. He made the sign of the Star mockingly. He unfastened his cloak and thrust it back to hang from his broad shoulders. The bright light glittered on the ornamented war harness of a star king. A great sword hung at his side, the pommel carved with the royal mark of Sarissa.

"They could help me," the warlock said querulously. "By the Star, they *should* help me—"

"Don't swear by the Star, Kelber," the star king said with mock sadness. "You'll be struck down." His cold eyes surveyed the clutter of forbidden machines. On Sarissa the mere possession of such engines of sin could mean death at the hands of a terrified mob. Perhaps, he was thinking in his icy, methodical way, it would be simplest merely to call the patrolmen.

The old man sat, confused in his mind. His folded hands trembled. He was trying to remember. It seemed to him that things had not always been this way. It seemed to him only a short time ago he had been a robust man, a seeker after the old knowledge, a strong man with a searching mind, impatient with the laws and the timid questings of the Navigators. But what had happened, he wondered. Where did it all go? How did I forget? How did I grow old?

The star king stepped to the center of the room and looked down at the incomplete thing on the rack. He prodded it with a booted foot. The wires trembled. There was no sign of life. He turned to look speculatively at Kelber. "What were your plans for *this*, I wonder."

The warlock rubbed his bony hands across his face and frowned. "Plans? What plans? I don't understand you."

"Three years ago you were told there was no need for this cyborg. Energy weapons are what're wanted. But you wasted your time on this—thing."

The old man grew suddenly very angry. "You— you and this thing, as you call it, are the same, Tallan. You remember that."

The star king shook his head. "You are old, Grandfather. You grow senile. You imagine things. How could such a thing be?" The mouth smiled, but the eyes remained cold, watchful.

The warlock shook his head and blinked his tired eyes. "Tallan. You remember. You *must* remember—"

Again, that slow and contemptuous shake of the head. "You only imagine it happened that way, old one. I am Sarissa—a star king. How could what you say be true?"

"Here, Tallan," the old man said pleadingly. "Here in this workshop—"

"No."

"Tallan?" A puzzled twist of the head.

"I said that you imagined it, Grandfather. I let you imagine it because it amused me. But tonight it does not amuse me."

Kelber felt his old heart flutter. He suddenly realized his danger.

Tallan said, "I warned Landro that you were an old fool. I told him that he would get no weapons from you." He smiled grimly. "You know only the *Book of Warls,* and there are no weapons there."

"I never claimed it," the warlock muttered. "The *Warls* tell of things that *were*. Men must find for themselves. I *know*—"

"What, exactly, do you know?" Tallan said scornfully. "Landro asked for weapons, and you spent his money on *this*." He pushed again at the racked, inert cyborg with a booted foot. "I should call the patrolmen."

The old man grew crafty. "That you'll never do— king." He came down hard on the last word, for he did remember now, he was sure that he remembered Tallan lying just there, on that same rack— When, how long ago? He couldn't recall, but it was so, and his voice filled with irony and emotion because Tallan, who wore the harness of a star king, who threatened his life, was not even a *man*.

The warleader's eyes narrowed speculatively.

The old man's arrogance increased, expanded dangerously. But he was too angry and confused to be prudent. "The people fear you," he said. "They call you The Unknown. But I know you, Tallan, star king, great warleader—*I* know you."

Tallan said thoughtfully, "Perhaps you do, Grandfather. Perhaps, after all, you do—"

The old warlock's mind veered wildly back to his obsession. "Then help me," he demanded heedlessly. "Tell Landro I need power—more equipment— Tell him I want—" He stopped suddenly because Tallan had moved across the room and stood over him now, towering, darkly menacing.

"The trouble with knowledge-seekers," Tallan said quietly, "is their fanaticism. They can't be controlled, and when that happens, old man, their usefulness is at an end. Sometimes they are even so unwise as to threaten their protectors."

The old warlock's breath began to come in short, labored gasps. It had been years since he had known real fear, and he could scarcely recognize it now. But his mouth was dry, and his body trembled as he shrank back, back, until his shoulders touched the cold stones of the wall.

"Every living thing," Tallan said, "has the instinct of self-preservation, the need to destroy what threatens it. *Every* living thing, Grandfather. You taught me that yourself. Do you remember?"

Kelber blinked. He could feel his ancient heart pounding and leaping within his chest like an imprisoned animal. Had he taught Tallan? Yes, of course he had. He could remember now the great naked shape stirring with first life, the first childlike weeks with a lifetime of knowledge to impart in six months, a year. He learned so quickly, so well, not like a human child at all. And there had been times when he had wished, with all his old man's human heart, that the cyborg could learn to love, to be a son, to be a man. But, of course, it never came to that. And he could recall the great strength, the power, and the training for war, and the slashing climb through the shattered ranks of the bandit captains who tried to hold Sarissa then. What chance had they against Tallan? Gods of space, what chance had *he,* Kelber, now?

Suddenly, the smell of the marshes was strong in his old nostrils, and life seemed very precious, even this doddering, failing life. "Tallan," he said shrilly, "Tallan—no—*no*—"

But the great warman had struck one strong blow with a fist of mail. The old man's head was flung back against the stones of the wall with a sickening sound of crushing bone.

For a time, Tallan stood unmoving, listening to the unnatural stillness. Then he touched the old man's throat, feeling for a pulse that no longer throbbed.

He picked up the warlock's body as though it weighed nothing and carried it to a straw pallet in the corner. He did not give it another glance.

Next he moved to the unfinished cyborg on the rack. He drew a blade of god-metal from his harness and swiftly opened the head. From the bloodless cavity, he took an oval object trailing hundreds of hair-thin wires. He cracked it open against the edge of an electrical cabinet. Inside the oval, racing through a maze of printed circuits and crystals, a tiny light flickered. He reversed his dagger, and using the pommel, he crushed the contents of the brain-egg. It took a long while, but presently the light faded and died out completely.

He dropped the two halves of the cyborg's brain

onto the stones of the floor and ground the crystal and plastic to bits beneath his heel. "Sleep long, brother," he murmured with an ironic half-smile.

He sheathed the dagger and drew his great sword of god-metal. For several minutes he walked methodically from one wired cabinet to another, smashing dials and controls, overturning equipment racks, savaging wiring until it hung in useless tangles from the ancient machines. In moments he destroyed the work of half a lifetime.

When he had finished, he turned to the book-laden tables, overturning them, spilling sheaves of priceless old manuscripts and diagrams over the flagstones. Then he took flint and god-metal from his pouch and struck a fire. When it was burning well, he smashed the light globes so that the room was illuminated only by the spreading flames, splashing and dancing on the old walls.

Without looking back now, he walked through the burning room to the doorway. He paused, listening. Satisfied that he was unobserved, he let himself out into the Street of Night, under Sarissa's dull and sullen sky. He carefully closed and locked the door behind him.

He was at the citadel walls before he heard the alarm being spread in the city. When he turned to look, the flames were dancing and sparking over the housetops. He listened to the growing uproar in the streets for a long while, feeling the strange emotion that was, for him, the counterpart of human satisfaction.

Chapter Three

Nyor, Nyor, city of sin
Dance with the warlocks
Let troubles begin
There they will gather the witches and kings
There let them be when the tocsin bell rings.

From the *Book of Warls*,
Interregnal period

Despite the destruction of the civil wars that shattered the First Empire and the repeated sackings of the capital during the dark time of the Interregnum, Nyor remained the greatest city on the home planet of the galaxy's only star-voyaging race. Glamiss Magnifico, though a native of Vyka, believed the ancient proverb: Who rules Nyor rules Earth. Who rules Earth rules the stars. *Thus Nyor became, after the Battle of Karma, the personal holding of the Vykan Galactons and the first city of the Second Stellar Empire.*

Nv. Julianus Mullerium, *The Age of the Star Kings*,
middle Second Stellar Empire period

29

TORQUAS Primus, Galacton, King of the Universe, Protector of the Faith, Defender of the Inner and Outer Marches, Commander of the Starfleets, Lord of Nyor, and Hereditary Warleader of Vyka, had a cold.

His eyes itched and burned; his throat was sore and his nose red and liquid. He was absolutely convinced that he burned with a high and possibly dangerous fever, despite assurances from his doctors that he was discomfited—nothing more.

Young Torquas had been cross all day, depressed and confined by his illness and by the rain that had been drenching Nyor for a week. The city, perched on its huge tel, seemed to huddle in the inclement weather. The boats on the river were docked and covered against the rain, the four million Nyori kept to their houses (for they had a superstitious dread of rainfall that dated back to the dawn of time when the blood-sickness was said to have fallen from the sky), and even the citadel grounds were deserted except for the Vykan guardsmen patrolling in their oiled leather capes and hoods. So Torquas kept to his rooms, annoyed by his companions and neglected by his wife.

Marlana had promised to call on him, and she had not. She hadn't sent the actors to amuse him as she had promised to do, either. She had not even come to question his physicians about his state of health—which was very bad, no matter what the stupid medics said.

It was even possible, Torquas thought grimly, that he might be close to death. He considered the masses of grieving Nyori, the yellow-draped monuments, the hovering starships and warmen with reversed weapons in his funeral train. There would be dirges for days, and the women of the household would cut their love-locks to burn on the star king's bier. Oh, it would be a fine sight! He remembered his father's funeral: far and away the most impressive pageant he could ever remember seeing. Only, if the funeral were his own, he would of course not see it—unless the priest-Navigators were right and he would be carried into Paradise in a great crystal starship from which he could see all the wonders of the Universe (of which he was undoubted king). Including, he supposed, his own great funeral.

Still, it might possibly be that he was suffering from something not quite fatal, in which case he would have to reprimand Marlana for her neglect as soon as he felt able.

He lay on his curtained bed, listening to the comings and goings of the two dozen courtiers who never left him. He was still rather morbidly considering his own death, but he concluded that it was very hard for anyone, even the Galacton, to come to grips with such a notion at the age of twelve years. Perhaps, when he became old enough to lead troops in battle, when he could actually see men die, he would be better able to cope with abstract death. Though when that remarkable day might come, he really did not know.

When his father, The Magnifico, was still alive, he remembered, he had at least been trained in the use of arms. But since the great king's departure for Paradise in the great crystal starship (*that* was really very hard to believe), there seemed no time for war games. Marlana insisted it was not fitting for the King of the Universe to spend his time in the armory swinging a wooden sword.

Marlana was a Vyk herself, and a relative—even a distant cousin—should understand that Torquas, as head of the family, should be a warrior. How else would he hold his lands, the hundreds of worlds so distant they could not be seen in Earth's sky even on the clearest of nights?

He sighed heavily and stirred on the furs that covered the Imperial bed.

He thought about his sister, the Princess Royal Ariane. He was very cross with Ariane, too. She had not been to see him in weeks. When he asked for her, Marlana and Landro said that she was still on Vyka, queening it on her estates. How dare Ariane go off-world without the Galacton's permission? What was the point of being King of the Universe if you couldn't even control your own sister?

He closed his eyes and listened to the people on the other side of the curtains. Avaric, the fat Altairi heir who was supposed to be Lord Chamberlain, was playing at Stars and Comets with Lady Constans, the governess. Privately, Torquas referred to Constans as Lady No because it was she who was in charge of his court education, which seemed to consist mainly of things the Galacton should *not* do. The pages were arguing about the ownership of a hunting peregrine, and something had happened to make Orrin, the Imperial equerry, cry. It sounded as though one of the nine Gentlemen Pensioners was comforting him. Torquas frowned petulantly. Who ever heard of a Galacton, a Commander of the Starfleets, with a five-year-old child for equerry? All because Orrin was bond-cousin to Landro, and Marlana insisted the post go to him as a member of the Veg clan.

Torquas had long ago decided he disliked all the members of the Veg family, Landro most of all. Marlana insisted Landro was wise and brave, but what really seemed to impress her most was that Landro was handsome. And, Torquas thought bleakly, too ambitious by half. He was enough Glamiss of Vyka's son to sense that. One day, he told himself, I'll challenge him to the Three Encounters with sword, flail, and dagger. It was a brave but futile thought. He knew it would never happen.

He could hear a flurry of activity in the outer chamber, and he wondered if someone was actually coming to see him. He hoped it would be Marlana, or at least the troupe of actors she promised.

He sat up and opened the curtains. Immediately, everyone in the room stood up. At first he had enjoyed making people do things of that sort. But now it only made him sulky because he knew he couldn't *really* make them do anything at all. Only Marlana or Landro could do that.

The fat Avaric said, "How may we serve you, King?"

Torquas scratched his pale face and blinked at the light. The day was silvery gray, and it was cold in the large, uncomfortable room. He signaled for Lady No to bring him a bed jacket. When she had settled it over his narrow shoulders, he asked, "What was Orrin crying about?"

The equerry blinked and stared sullenly at his sovereign. "It was nothing, sir," Lady No said. "Lord Avaric took a sweet from him."

The Lord Chamberlain, who was fifteen and had a bad complexion from overeating, looked daggers at the governess.

"You're far too fat already, Avaric," the Galacton said. "If you don't stop eating so, I shall have to send you back to the Western Sea." Avaric's family held the Oahu Islands in the center of Earth's great Western Ocean, an isolated estate that Avaric loathed for its warm weather, disturbing to his plump constitution.

"What's happening outside?" Torquas asked. "Has someone come to see me?"

"Soldiers, sir," Lady No said. "Warmen."

"Of course there are warmen there," Torquas said impatiently. "There always are."

"But a great many, sir," Avaric said. "A full squadron."

"Outside my door?" Torquas said curiously. "Open. Let me see."

Avaric signaled to one of the pages, and the boy swung the heavy god-metal door. The draft from the gallery made the tapestries sway. Beyond the doorway stood two ranks of Vegan Imperials in full war gear. Their gilded conical helmets bore the mark of Landro's own division.

Torquas swung his bare feet over the side of the high bed.

"Oh, sir. You shouldn't," Lady Constans exclaimed. "The doctors said most distinctly that you should stay in bed."

Torquas ignored her and said, "Bring the squadron officer to me, Avaric."

The fat Lord Chamberlain retired and presently returned with a hard-faced young warman, who knelt at the Galacton's bedside.

"Leader," he said, using the formal Vegan title. Torquas felt a twinge of irritation. Vegans were a gritty lot, always preferring their own out-land ways to the manners of Nyor.

"What's happening," Torquas demanded. "Why is your squadron outside my door?"

"Orders, Leader," the warman said.

"The Galacton is addressed as King," Lady No said severely. "Or Lord, if you prefer. Never as Leader."

The warman turned cold eyes on the governess. "I am a Vegan, Lady," he said.

Torquas made a gesture of impatience. "Never mind all that. I want to know what is happening. Are we being attacked?" He half hoped that the answer would be yes. To be attacked would be exciting. Maybe he could lead his own division into battle and make Marlana proud. "Is there trouble, warman?"

"A precaution, sir."

"I don't understand. A precaution against what?"

The courtiers in the room began to murmur amongst themselves. The squadron officer and the armed men in the gallery made them uneasy.

"We have orders to protect you, sir. That is all."

"Who gave such orders?" Torquas asked.

"The Empress-Consort."

Torquas rubbed his reddened nose. "Who am I being protected *from*, warman?"

The officer got to his feet without permission and said, "There is a Rhadan starship entering the atmosphere. That is all I know."

Torquas turned to Avaric. "What's happening here? Are we at war with Rhada? I have been told nothing about this."

Avaric, wide-eyed, shook his head stupidly. "I've heard of no war, King."

Lady No was not about to be intimidated by the cold-eyed Vegan. She stationed herself in front of him and declared, "There is no conceivable reason the arrival of a Rhadan starship should cause alarm in Nyor. In the first place, there are troops enough on the East Coast to defend the capital against a dozen starships. And in the second place, Kier of Rhada is as loyal as any star king in the Empire."

Torquas nodded. "Kier was one of my father's best warleaders."

The warman shrugged. "Nevertheless, Leader, I have my orders. A Rhadan vessel will soon be landing, and I have been told to protect you."

"What nonsense," Lady No said severely.

"When will the ship land, when?" Orrin cried excitedly.

"Within the hour," the officer said.

"I want to go see," Torquas said suddenly.

The officer looked uncomfortable. "My orders say that you must remain here, sir."

Torquas dropped from the bed and stood, barefoot and very young, before the armed soldier. "Who gave that order, warman?" he asked with a suddenly acquired dignity.

"The warleader, sir."

"Landro?"

"Sir."

"And who am _I_, warman?"

The soldier looked unhappy. "The Galacton, sir."

Torquas studied the hard face and realized that the officer would not obey him. It would be foolish and perhaps even dangerous to attempt to force obedience.

Torquas drew a breath and said, "Leave me."

"Sir." The warman saluted and withdrew.

"Avaric," Torquas said. "I want to get dressed."

Lady Constans made gestures of disapproval, clucking about the Galacton's health and the instructions of the doctors. But when she saw the boy's face, she grew silent.

Avaric and the Gentlemen Pensioners helped the Galacton to dress. Torquas wished that he had proper war harness to wear, but there was none. He had outgrown his old war gear, and Marlana had done nothing about providing him with new.

He had finished washing himself in a basin held by a page when Marlana was announced. The Empress-Consort, dressed in a short gown of Vykan yellow, approached through the crowd of bowing courtiers. At her back came Landro, his tall and slender figure resplendent in court dress. He carried only ceremonial weapons, and he was not dressed for war. His hair was long, in the Vegan mode, and caught at the nape of his neck with a silver clasp. Torquas did not like Vegan styles. His father, he remembered, thought them perverse, and now so did he. But Marlana was beautiful, with a narrow, finely made face and short black Vykan hair worn close to her small, shapely head. Her hazel eyes reminded Torquas of his dimly remembered mother.

His wife inclined her head formally. Among Vyks, a wife did not bow to her husband. She extended her hand, and Torquas kissed it as he had been taught to do.

"I hope you are well, husband," Marlana said. "I had not thought to find you out of bed."

"What's happening, Marlana?" Torquas demanded impatiently. "Why are the warmen here?"

"Only for your protection, loved one. There is a hostile starship in the atmosphere."

"When did the Rhad become hostile? Why wasn't I told of it?"

"Who mentioned the Rhad to you, husband?" Marlana asked evenly.

"The officer. The officer out there in the gallery."

Marlana glanced at Landro, who nodded assent and left the room. Torquas could hear voices in the gallery and the formal posting of weapons.

"The officer should not have said it is a Rhadan

starship," Marlana said soothingly. "We are not yet
sure. But we must be cautious, husband. You are the
Galacton."

Landro returned and said to Marlana, "He's been
relieved."

Torquas looked from his wife to the warleader. He
wished that it didn't always seem they were alone
together when they were speaking to him. Perhaps it
was that they were grown up and he was not. But he
was, after all, King of the Universe. "Well," he said
with some irritation, *"is* it the Rhad?"

"All this is a precaution, King," Landro said con-
fidently. "Nothing more."

"Kier of Rhada was my father's friend," Torquas
said, rubbing at his nose and wondering how one could
be dignified with a head cold.

"You haven't seen the recent dispatches, loved one,"
Marlana said. "His messages have gone from insolent
to threatening. And now, suddenly, here he seems to
be—perhaps with a starship full of warmen. We must
take care. He isn't called The Rebel for nothing, husband."

Torquas's composure was beginning to break. He
didn't understand why he had been told nothing of all
this. Yet Marlana and Landro never told him anything
political. They said he was too young to be troubled.
"Why be Galacton if you can't rely on your loyal
subjects?" she said. Somehow, Torquas doubted that
his father would ever have let anyone do things in the
Imperial name without telling him about it. But then,
at twelve, Glamiss Magnifico had been leading armies
in war on Vyka.

"Well, *is* it Kier or isn't it?" he demanded.

"It *might be,"* Marlana said, brushing a fall of hair
away from his forehead. "The ship is only just out of

Earth orbit, loved one. But we simply cannot take any chances with the Rhad—*if* it is the Rhad."

Torquas shook his head in confusion. He wondered why it was that Marlana could make things so very difficult to understand.

"Well, I want to see the starship land," he said almost plaintively.

Marlana glanced once again at Landro and inclined her head quizzically. "I see no objection to that, do you, Warleader?"

"None, Queen," Landro said.

"You shall see it, then, husband," Marlana said. "From the Empire Tower."

Torquas felt a sudden inner chill. "The tower?" The Empire Tower was the most ancient structure in the city. Its lower levels lay deep within the tel, five hundred feet or more. And its upper levels had been destroyed and rebuilt times beyond counting in the turbulent history of Nyor. Since Interregnal times it had been used to house political prisoners. It reeked of cybs and demons.

Marlana smiled and ran her hand gently through the boy's hair. "The view is best from there. You can see far beyond the river. And you will be safer there than here if there should be any fighting." She drew a folded parchment from her gown. "But first I need your name on this paper," she said. "It is an Imperial warrant for the commander of that starship—whoever he may be."

Torquas sighed and leaned against her. "Must he be arrested? If it is Kier, I mean?"

"No one may be permitted to land at Nyor with a vessel filled with troops, husband. You remember Father Glamiss made that the law."

"But Kier of Rhada—"

"The law is the law, loved one. You must enforce it."

Torquas nodded agreement. Marlana was right, of course. Grownups were always right. It made being King of the Universe difficult. He took the paper to an escritoire and wrote across the bottom: Torquas the First, G. He liked signing state documents that way. Of course, Marlana could have signed it herself, as regent. But he was pleased that she wanted him to put his royal name to this one, though he would be sorry if it got Kier into trouble. Still, he had no right to come dropping down on the Imperial capital with an army—

Marlana took the paper from him and said, "Now I'll have the warmen take you to see the starship land."

Landro was smiling strangely at the doorway. The courtiers, those old enough to understand what was happening, looked uncomfortable. Landro opened the door and signaled for an officer. The hard-faced Vegan had gone.

The officer presented himself before Landro and saluted. Torquas wondered why he had not come directly to him. Wasn't he Galacton?

Landro said, "Conduct the Lord Torquas to the Empire Tower so that he may see the Rhadan vessel land. Guard him well. The engineer of the tower will know where the view is best."

"The top, Marlana," Torquas said excitedly. "The very top."

Marlana looked at Landro and smiled. "The top, Warleader," she agreed.

For some reason Torquas could not understand, Lady Constans began to weep. She put her arms about Torquas and held him, to his embarrassment. She looked at the Empress-Consort and said, "Oh, Queen—he's not well, he's ill—"

Torquas drew away from her and said, "I am perfectly fit." He lifted his chin and said to the Vegan warman, "Hurry. I do not want to miss it."

Marlana stood in silence as the boy and Landro's warmen marched off down the gallery. She turned to look coldly at the courtiers, thinking contemptuously that not one of them except old Constans had raised a hand or even voiced a protest. "All of you," she said, "leave us."

When they had gone, leaving her alone with Landro, she took the Instrument of Abdication from her gown and read the formal words written in the ancient Vykan language.

Landro brushed the back of her neck with his knuckles gently, familiarly. "You have my admiration, Queen," he said.

Marlana broke into laughter. "Queen of the Universe, Landro," she said.

Landro giggled. The sound disturbed Marlana and irritated her. There was a streak of hysteria in the man, a tension that it seemed to her might one day bring him suddenly to disaster. Marlana mistrusted flawed tools, but for the moment there was only Landro at hand, and he must be steadied and used.

She walked to the gallery and stood by the high, narrow windows looking at the gray sky through which the Rhadan starship must descend to Nyor.

She thrust the document into her breast and turned. "I shall change into royal red," she said, "the color of kings, to greet our warlike visitor, The Rebel of Rhada."

Chapter Four

*—therefore the tactics of defense during landing op-
erations of capital ships is dependent upon the expected response from enemy high-energy weapons.
With meson screens fully extended, the deployment of
infantry is limited by the metric-ton capacity of the
standard Mark XVII Matter Transceiver: that is to
say, units of battalion strength and 18.6 seconds. Starships equipped with the newer Mark XX Transceiver
may deploy units of regimental size at inter—*

Golden Age fragment found at Tel-Paris, Earth
(believed to be part of
an Imperial military field manual)

*On grounding after planetfall, the commander of war-
men seeking to insure the safety of his holy vessel will
order the portals opened only after his cavalry screen
has been formed. The mounted warmen must then
move with swiftness, establishing a perimeter and at-
tacking any stone- or missile-throwing devices within
range of the vessel. Meanwhile, the Navigator must
be alert to danger, prepared instantly to lift the vessel*

to a height of no less than one hundred meters. Simultaneously, the crew must make ready to support the cavalry screen with heavy stones and fire spears from the keel bays.

Prince Fernald, *On Tactics,*
early Second Stellar Empire period

AGAINST the gray sky, the Rhadan starship made a thousand-meter void of darkness. Its descent toward the East Coast of the northern continent was cautious, with many hovering halts. The forces that drove the ship so swiftly through space were held in check now, and the air around it glowed with a pale blue radiance, ionizing the cloud layers so that the moisture froze into rime ice on the dark god-metal of the immense blind hull.

In the broad corridor leading to the port-side valve, a squadron of Rhadan cavalry was forming, the warmen tightening the harness on their nervously stepping mounts. The horses were of Rhadan stock, slenderlimbed, with padded and clawed feet. These were said to be descendants of the horses of ancient Earth, brought to Rhada millennia ago in cold tubes and fitted to the rigors of Rhadan life by some warlock's magic called *mutation.*

The animals were accustomed to star travel, but they were partially telepathic and could sense from their masters the possibility of fighting soon. Their extended claws rasped on the metal of the deck plates, and they snorted the few words of their rudimentary language to one another: "Blood!" "Battle!" "Anger!" Occasionally, they would nip nervously at the mailed fighting men, their carnivorous teeth slipping harmlessly from the scales of iron. The men would cuff

them back, curbing their eagerness and talking to them
half in love, half in anger.

In the armory, Kier of Rhada's weaponeers har-
nessed him for battle. His shirt of mail was washed
with silver, and it gleamed in the torchlight. Before
him, in a semicircle, stood Nevus, the Lieutenant-
General, Kalin, and Cavour, the warlock. All were
armed and armored.

Nevus, a heavy-set and battle-scarred veteran of
the Rim wars, was scowling at his youthful leader. "I
still don't like the plan, Kier. It's far too risky."

"On the contrary," the young man said, clasping
the final buckle of his weapons harness, "it's the least
risky way of handling a bad situation. Cavour?"

The warlock's bearded face was grave. "Yes.
Though I still suggest a fast flight to Sarissa instead."

Kier shook his head. "A last resort only."

"You may be making your last choice right now,"
Nevus growled. "At least take me with you."

Kier said, "I'll need you at the landing ground."

Kalin, the priest-Navigator, spoke for the first time.
He did not want to presume to advise his cousin, who
was much more experienced in war and intrigue than
he, but he felt it his right as a Rhad to say, "What
good will it do us to hold the starship and the landing
ground if we lose you, Kier?"

"What the boy says is true," Nevus said. "Listen
to him, King."

From the shadows, Gret spoke. "No man goes adrift
on a dangerous sea without purpose—and a thin line
to the land."

"Thin line. Yes, I will agree to that," Nevus said.
"We've barely a squadron aboard."

"All of Rhada couldn't take the capital, Nevus," the young star king said. "Nor would I want it so even if it were possible."

"And they call you Rebel," Nevus grumbled.

"It is decided," Kier said, in a tone to end argument.

Nevus turned to Cavour. "Then remember your best spells, Warlock."

Cavour showed his teeth in a smile. He liked Nevus, who was a brave soldier but a lifetime scoffer at the old knowledge. "Maybe one day I'll produce something to impress you. An exploding missile or a ship to travel under the sea. But it won't be today. Once they have us in the citadel, we'll be in God's hands."

Kalin instinctively made the sign of the Star, but Nevus only pulled his beard and muttered, "In Landro's hands, you mean."

"Enough," Kier said. "Now listen to me."

The other fell silent.

"We shall land at the south end of the tel, where the slope is steep behind us. I shall take only Cavour with me. The rest you know. Nevus—hold the landing ground. Without fighting, if you can, but hold it. If we have not returned in eight hours, put the men aboard the ship." He took his cousin's shoulder. "Then we will be in your care, Kalin."

"Can the thing be done, though?" Nevus asked.

"Kalin can do it," Kier replied.

Kalin inclined his head and prayed that his skill be sufficient to succeed at what many said was impossible. Kier, with his quick instinct, said, "There is no better ship handler among the Navigators. I have no fear."

Kalin swallowed the dryness in his throat and said

formally, "It shall be done, King."

From the shadows came the thrumming of Gret's music. "If Ariane is there, so will Erit be. I should like to meet with one of my own kind again. So shall I have to stay here without you, King, while you go adventuring?"

"What is your pleasure, Master Gret?" Kier asked with half a frown.

"I might be useful," said the Vulk.

"So you might," Kier said speculatively. "On a journey into the unknown, the unknowable may serve."

"You do me honor, King," Gret said with a secret smile.

One of the novice Navigators appeared with a position report. "We are through the cloud deck, sir."

"Are we over the Eastern Sea?" Kalin asked.

"Yes, Brother Kalin."

Kalin said to his cousin, "I will go now." Kier watched him go, thinking that the lives of all might soon depend on the young priest's skill and piety. He accepted his helmet from an armorer and smiled at his lieutenants. "Then, gentlemen, I do think it is time."

The Rhadan starship hovered for a time low over the southern tip of Manhat Island, above a section of the tel that covered much of the ancient city of Nyor. The ground was level here, dropping steeply to the shores of the confluence of the two rivers. To the north, no more than three kilometers from where the great ship would touch ground, two battalions of Vegan Imperials were issuing in battle order from the gate of the wall that cut across the island. The wall, useless now for defense, had been built in the last years of the Interregnum. It was falling into decay, but it served to divide the spaces left open for starship landings from the tangled streets and alleyways of Imperial Nyor.

Normally, starships landed closer to the walls. But Kalin allowed his huge hull to settle slowly to Earth at a point so near the steep talus of the tel that it would be virtually impossible to surround her. On the crumbling wall, he could see arbalests and catapults, but he was reasonably certain that even the huge and cleverly designed Imperial machines had not the range to reach his chosen landing site with missiles.

A rain was falling as the starship actually touched ground. The flicker of ionization in the air around her faded, and the god-metal keel sank deeply into the soil.

The port-side valve dilated, and from the dark opening galloped two wings of Rhadan cavalry, short lances set in holders, god-metal flails ready across the riders' saddle-bows. The horses wore no headgear, for they were guided by their sensing of their riders' wills. They moved silently and with great precision and far more swiftly than the Vegan troops issuing from the city, who were mounted on scaly Vegan animals that had been mutated to grow armor and had thus sacrificed speed for virtual imperviousness to attack.

The Rhadans quickly established a defensive perimeter about the starship. At a command from Nevus, now stationed in the center of the circle, Rhadan engineers rolled forth two missile casters consisting of five oversized crossbows loaded with god-metal quarrels. These were emplaced ten meters on either side of the starship's open portal.

The commander of the Vegan warmen watched these hostile activities and made a tactical decision. He deployed his troops in attack columns, advanced them to within half a kilometer of the waiting Rhadans, and halted them there.

His orders had been to take Kier of Rhada into his custody and escort him, without delay or public display, to the citadel. Clearly, this would now be impossible without a bloody encounter—and his orders did not cover this possibility. The Nyori had seen the starship landing, and they were gathering in great numbers about the wall, even pouring out onto the landing ground. Kier of Rhada was a great favorite among the people of Nyor; they remembered him as a trusted captain of The Magnifico's, one of the men who had brought a semblance of peace to the home planet after generations of war. They recognized the harness of the troops from the starship as Rhadan and had begun to wave and cheer. Already, there were some hundreds of Nyori braving the rain; the word was spreading, and more were coming to join the throng. A battle with the Rhadans would most certainly be "a public display," and it would undoubtedly cause considerable "delay." Thus, the Vegan commander acted as soldiers have acted for twenty thousand years. He bucked the problem along to higher authority by sending for Landro, the Imperial warleader.

At this point, Kier of Rhada, flanked by Cavour and Gret—the Vulk absurdly resplendent atop a Rhadan war mare—emerged from the starship and rode silently to the edge of the Rhadan perimeter. Immediately, the portal half closed behind them, so that even a concerted rush by the Imperials could not overrun the starship. The people of Nyor had begun to shout greetings to the popular young man known

as The Rebel, but the obviously grim meaning of the
Rhadan deployment was not lost on them, and they
stirred uneasily.

For the better part of thirty minutes, the fighting
men on the landing ground sat their mounts in silence,
Rhadans gripping their flails, Vegans with their axes
to hand.

As the tension mounted, Kier murmured a word to
Gret, and the Vulk smiled broadly and took up his
instrument.

He began to play a lilting air, the melody of a song
of the people, a ballad about a Vegan star king of a
century ago whose doings were still the subject of
much ribaldry.

The people cheered, and the Vegan troopers smiled.
Pride in the amorous doings of their nobility was a
very Vegan characteristic. Less warlike than the spartan Rhadans, the Imperials began to call out to the
visitors in friendly terms, to the embarrassment of
their frustrated commander.

Gret, playing the fool, made his mare prance and
step in time to the music, and the people cheered more
loudly, relieved at this small sign of nonwarlike intent
on the part of the Rhadans.

Sitting beside the young star king, Cavour said
quietly, "I see what he meant by saying he might be
useful."

"I expect more than this from Gret," Kier said.

Cavour raised his eyes to the activity atop the wall.
Even at this distance he could see that the war engines
were fully manned. And now a smaller but far more
resplendent body of troops was issuing from the city.

Like a wave, silence spread across the crowd of
Nyori. Gret's music ended as the people turned to
look at the Imperial warleader's bodyguard cantering

toward the first rank of Vegan Imperials. At the head of the guardsmen rode Landro.

Kier noted that he was in court dress and not in war harness. He murmured to Cavour, "I may have misjudged him."

"As a bird misjudges a snake, Kier."

Landro paused for a word with the Imperial commander and then rode on alone, the scales of his Vegan horse glistening wetly in the silvery light of the afternoon.

Kier moved his mount through the lines to meet him. The two men stopped with their animals' heads only a meter apart, and the Rhadan mare laid her ears back and bared her teeth at her distant, distant relative. She twisted her head to look at her master, rolling her eyes. "Kill?" she asked. Kier soothed her, patting her arching, sweating neck, and told her no.

"What nasty beasts you Rhadans keep, cousin," Landro said.

Kier, who only by the greatest stretch of genealogical imagination could be considered a cousin of Landro's, replied, "They suit us, Leader." He spoke in Vegan dialect, rather than Imperial, as a courtesy to the Veg.

Landro accepted the compliment and said, "Welcome to Nyor. But why all the warlike preparations?" He smiled dryly. "Have you come to conquer us with a squadron of warmen?"

"I came because I was called, Landro. I landed as Rhadans always land. We Rim-world people have learned to be cautious, not warlike. Is the Emperor well?"

Landro inclined his head. "Well and waiting to receive you."

"And is that why I was met by a regiment of Imperials?" Kier asked quietly.

"These are troubled times, cousin. Any starship landing so far from the walls is apt to be met with—precautionary measures."

"And now that you know it is only the loyal Rhad, you'll withdraw your troops, of course."

"The Emperor will give the order himself, no doubt," Landro said with a strange and nervous laugh.

Here, then, was the moment of truth, thought Kier. To refuse to accompany Landro would be to confirm himself indeed as The Rebel of Rhada. Caution and deep suspicions of the Imperial urged him to withdraw to the security of his starship and depart. But to do so would mean rebellion, war between Rhada and the Empire, and possibly the premature death of all that Kier's father Aaron, Glamiss the Magnificent, Kier himself, and half a hundred loyal star kings had sought to create: a rebirth of Empire, perhaps the foundations of another Golden Age.

"I am here to escort you to Torquas and the Regent, cousin," Landro said.

Kier's war mare pranced nervously, showing her teeth.

"A moment, Landro," Kier said, and turned his mount to canter back to the Rhadan perimeter. Nevus, dismounted, walked reluctantly to his stirrup and looked up, anxiety on his bearded face.

"We will go with him now, Nevus," Kier said. "You have your instructions."

Nevus touched his king's mailed wrist. "May God protect you, sir."

Kier signaled Cavour and Gret to join him, and the three trotted their animals through the lines to where Landro waited, now flanked by a wing of his guardsmen.

"My greetings, Cavour," Landro said. He did not speak to Gret. The Vegans had exterminated all their Vulks a generation ago, and their prejudice made them suffer in the presence of the strange creatures.

The guardsmen formed files on either side, and the party cantered through the massed Imperials and Nyori to the city gate.

Cavour said, "Think what it must be, Gret, actually to live on this tel, where every foot of ground must hold some ancient secret."

The Vulk, riding close behind his young star king, turned his blind, wise face to the warlock and said, "Yes, many things are buried here. Mysteries and artifacts—and trusting men."

Cavour grunted. He could hear Landro nattering foolishly to Kier, giggling his tremulous laugh. Behind them, the armored ranks of the Vegan Imperials closed so that when the warlock turned to look, he could see the great hull of their starship seemingly afloat on a sea of conical helmets and menacing spears.

Chapter Five

In the second decade of the Second Stellar Empire, stealth and political chicanery contrived to enlarge the Vegan garrison of the capital to a point where Landrite troops were very nearly Praetorian in their influence. Surrounded by the Veg, the Vykan Dynasty stood in mortal danger.

Nv. Julianus Mullerium, *The Age of the Star Kings,*
middle Second Stellar Empire period

Who has a Vegan for a friend has no need of an enemy.

Proverb, early Second Stellar Empire period

THE ride through the streets of Nyor began as a progress, but once within the walls, the Rhadan sensed the change. The way was lined with Vegan Imperials, far more than courtesy demanded. And these were skirmishers, light-armored men, each with a drawn crossbow across his saddle.

The people of Nyor, who had cheered Kier and his party outside the gate, now stood silently, sensing that they might be witnesses to some great treachery, but helpless to prevent it.

The rain fell in a steady, gentle drizzle out of a high gray sky, and Cavour murmured, "This is headsman's weather, King."

If Landro heard, he gave no sign.

Kier said, "Do you need so many troops to control the Nyori, Landro?"

"Why would you think that, Kier?" the Veg said easily. "We only seek to do you honor."

"I'm touched," Kier replied dryly.

The procession moved slowly through the tangled ancient slums of the city, where the buildings were decayed blocks of glass and plastic and rusted godmetal, toward the new town, where stone houses and the massive cylindrical form of the citadel dominated the narrow, crooked streets.

Gret whispered to Kier, "They will take us when we enter the citadel."

Kier replied in Rhadan, which Landro did not speak. "Are you certain?"

The Vulk shrugged. "I sense it so."

Cavour said, "You knew it when we put our heads into the mouth of the beast."

"I had hoped it would be different. We are in the hands of God," Kier said.

"We are in the hands of Landro," Cavour remarked acidly. "Which is not at all the same thing. Do we fight?"

Kier shook his head.

Cavour said, "It is just as well. I am a poor swordsman."

Kier half smiled at his warlock. No man could doubt his courage, though warlocks were not famed as fighting men. And then, for reasons that he could not imagine, the young star king found himself thinking of Ariane, that princess he had not seen for many years. What had become of her, he wondered. If there was, in fact, treachery and treason everywhere, could the transgressors have allowed her to live?

Landro was pointing at the new weapons on the flat roofs of the citadel. They were stone throwers of a new design, with slings loaded with what seemed to be thousands of pieces of jagged god-metal. Each war engine commanded an avenue of approach to the tiered residence of the Galacton.

"The designs of a warlock named Kelber," Landro said conversationally.

The name meant nothing to Kier. He said, "What enemy are you expecting, Landro? It seems those catapults were meant to be used against your own people."

"The Nyori are an unruly lot."

Kier studied the shrapnel-loaded machines of death. *That* unruly? This city seems more a war camp than the capital of an empire."

"The times are troublesome, cousin," Landro said. "Surely you've heard."

"Times are always troublesome. But on Rhada we don't arm against our own people. I wonder if you really do in Nyor."

"I say it, Kier," Landro said with growing coldness.

"Then it must be so."

Landro laughed suddenly. "On the word of a Veg."

Cavour raised his eyes to the wet sky, and Gret made a chuckling sound.

They had reached the gate to the Citadel. It stood open, and within the first courtyard Kier could see still more Vegan troops with crossbows. The Vyks of the Imperial guard were nowhere to be discovered. It was obvious that Landro, as commander of the garrison, had sent them all elsewhere.

The cavalcade rode into the yard, and the gate swung closed behind them. Kier raised his eyes to the top of the wall and saw Marlana standing there, cloaked against the rain. Then, not knowing why he did it at such a time, he looked even higher, to the narrow window of the round tower dominating the courtyard. He had a flashing glimpse of a young, narrow face framed in straight black hair—a Vykan face behind an X of god-metal bars. Was it Ariane? He had no time to consider, for Gret said clearly, "It happens *now*, King."

Kier wheeled his mare to face Landro just as he heard the twang and whir of crossbows. The three Rhadan mounts screamed in pain and fury and went down under a hail of quarrels. Kier struck the ground painfully, one leg caught beneath his murdered horse. Gret and Cavour were down as well, sprawled on the wet stones of the prison yard.

His war-trained reflexes brought the young star king to his feet instantly, sword bared in his hand. He had said they were not to fight, but his instincts demanded it. On the wall a second rank of crossbowmen raised their weapons.

"Wait!" Landro commanded.

The three Rhadans stood together at bay while their animals twitched and died miserably behind them. Kier felt a sick fury at the way it had been done. He had expected betrayal, but the form of it left him half maddened with rage.

Landro said, "Put down your weapons. There is no need for you to die."

Kier did not trust himself to speak. Now he knew what he had thought he must know, but he had bought the knowledge at the price of a fine horse and his freedom. His, Cavour's, and Gret's. God help them then if the plan so carefully made with Nevus and Kalin failed to work.

"You are under arrest for treason and conspiracy, Kier of Rhada," Marlana called. "Don't make us kill you where you stand."

Kier raised his sword and said bitterly, "I had this weapon from your husband's father, Marlana. I promised never to raise it against the Empire." He brought it down across his knee with all his strength and shattered the god-metal. Then he threw the two pieces from him, ringing on the stones. "But there are other swords, Queen!"

Cavour, who was, as he had said, no swordsman, dropped his weapon readily enough and murmured to Kier, "But why *don't* they kill us and have done with it?"

"They will send you and me to the tower," Gret murmured. "I cannot sense what they intend for Kier."

"Is that all you sense?" Kier spoke in a swift, low voice. "Quickly!"

"Erit is near," the Vulk said, "and still free."

Landro shouted a command, the Vegans closed in, crossbows ready. "The sorcerer and the Vulk-thing to the Empire Tower. Take The Rebel to the Empress's apartment."

Kier looked up at Marlana. Empress? He had expected treachery and had provided for it. But he had not foreseen high treason and the downfall of a king. Even the Rebel's imaginings had not gone so far as that.

Was Torquas still alive? he wondered. Had Marlana dared to murder the living symbol of the Vykan Dynasty? And Ariane? What of her? Gret said Erit lived, and he himself thought he had seen Ariane at the tower window. But was it truly she, or did the daughter of The Magnifico lie this minute in some unmarked grave on some forgotten planet half the galaxy away?

"Cavour," he said urgently in the Rhad tongue. "If I am not with you when Kalin's time comes, you must not wait." He silenced the warlock's protest with a gesture. "You must reach Sarissa at all costs now. The star kings must know what has happened here. I command it."

There was no time for more. The Vegans separated them roughly. Cavour watched, with uncertain heart, as his young king was led off between ranks of armed warmen. The warlock's courage faltered then, but only for a moment. If things had suddenly become much worse than he could have foreseen, then his responsibility to the Empire—and to his young master— was simply that much greater. "Events test the man," old Aaron used to say. Cavour felt the mailed hands of the guards close on his arms. No one touched the Vulk. Instead, they prodded him ahead at the point of a sword. In the rain-misted distance, Cavour could see the gloomy megalith of the Empire Tower, a symbol of death—and hope.

Chapter Six

What must the King do now? Must he submit?
The King shall do it. Must he be deposed?
The King shall be contented. Must he lose
The name of king?

> Attributed to one William Shakespeare,
> a Tudor propagandist of the pre-Golden Age.
> Fragment found at Tel-Avon, Earth

If a king be taken, let him die
If a king be murdered, let him lie
For power is in the edge of a sword
And a helpless king is no man's lord.

> From the *Book of Warls*,
> Interregnal period

TORQUAS stood at the rubbled parapet of the Empire Tower looking down at the vast panorama of Manhat spread out a kilometer below him. He stood heedless of the rain, his cold forgotten, half frightened by the

61

sheerness of the drop before him and yet excited by
the scene far below.

Behind him stood Janver of Florida, the stone-
faced giant who was the engineer of the tower. And
at Janver's side stood the captain of the Vegan detachment that had brought the Galacton to this high
and dreary place. The two men talked together in low
voices, glancing occasionally at the narrow back of
the boy at the railing. The Vegan, his face half hidden
by the god-metal nosepiece of his helmet, was speaking urgently, and each word seemed to make even
harder the granite-colored eyes of the burly Floridan.

Janver shook his head and said raspingly, "I will
not do it. Not without written warrant, warman. There's
an end to it."

Once again the Vegan showed the paper in his
mailed fist. "By the Veg, you have it *here*. I've shown
it to you!"

"You've shown me nothing I want to see."

"The warleader's seal. His orders, Engineer."

The Floridan looked once again at the boy and then
far out over the intervening distance to where the
Rhadan starship lay grounded at the south end of the
island. He folded his massive executioner's arms and
said, "I take my orders only from the Regent. Only
from her. It is the law."

The Vegan captain controlled his anger. "There is
no *time*, Engineer."

"I will not surrender my post, warman—not for a
hundred scraps of paper from the Veg. Floridans have
manned the tower for two hundred years. No out-
world toy soldier takes over here. That ends it." He
stepped forward to fasten the rain cape more securely
about the boy's shoulders. "Here, sir. Keep covered
up now."

Torquas turned his head to look up at the massive man and smiled. "Look there, Engineer. The Rhadans have formed a Parthian circle. Do you know what that is? I do, Engineer. My father taught me when I was a little boy."

"Tell me, sir," the big man said with gruff gentleness. He glanced back at the Vegan as the boy rambled on excitedly. The Veg was scowling as he thrust Landro's rescript into his gauntlet and stepped inside to where his squadron was waiting.

"It's a cavalry circle, you see," Torquas was saying. "In action they gallop around and around, shooting with their bows at the enemy. It makes them very hard to hit, and they can move the circle anywhere they want to go. Do you know why they call it a *Parthian* circle, Engineer?"

"No, I do not, King." The engineer of the tower spoke respectfully. His family had served the Galactons since The Magnifico's time.

"I don't either," Torquas said, turning back to watch the Rhad starship. "My father didn't tell me that." He stood up very straight and added, "But the Rhad are the best soldiers in the Empire. I guess they could beat the Veg if they fought."

"The Veg are your soldiers, too, sir," the Floridan said grudgingly.

"That's so," said the boy, shivering slightly in the wind that blew the fine rain against his face.

"You had best come inside, sir," Janver said.

"Not yet. Look. The Rhad are moving their arbalests back inside the starship. I suppose there will be no fight."

It was as he said. On the plain at the south end of the tel, the Rhadan warmen were slowly contracting their circle of held ground, and a wing of men were

wrestling the light artillery back through the valve
into the interior of the vessel. The Vegan Imperials,
who still formed ranks across the avenue to the city
gate, made no move to advance on the Rim-worlders.

Suddenly, from within the building, came the clash
of weapons and the sound of shouting. The engineer
made swiftly for the doorway, but by the time he had
reached the threshold, three of his Floridans lay dead
on the ferro-concrete floor, their weapons only half
drawn. Four Vegan warmen menaced him with their
crossbows, and from the guardroom immediately below came the sounds of surprised men fighting for
their lives—and losing. The Veg were racing through
the tower, decimating the largely ceremonial garrison
of the tower's upper levels.

Janver roared furiously and yanked his sword from
its scabbard only to have it shot out of his hand by a
well-aimed crossbow quarrel. He stood, rocking with
rage and the pain of his wounded hand, while the
Vegan officer strode past him to take the boy.

Torquas was badly frightened; he had never seen
dead troopers before, nor had he ever seen blood. But
he was Galacton, and as the Veg touched him, he
found his courage and struck out, bruising his naked
fist against the warman's helmet.

"That's the star king you're manhandling, you Vegan pig! the Floridan yelled, outraged by the act of
lèse-majesté and thrusting forward to intervene.

The Vegan signaled one of his men. "Kill him,"
he said.

The Veg warman brought the engineer down with
a quarrel between the shoulder blades. The big Floridan struck the floor heavily and was still.

Torquas fought to hold back the tears, but he could
not. The Vegan officer gathered him in, and for a

dreadful moment the boy thought the man was about to shove him over the parapet. But he only held him so that he could not struggle and carried him inside.

The Veg released the boy and gave a command in Vegan. "Take him down into the tel."

Torquas drew back against the wall and said in a shaky voice, "I am the Galacton, warmen." His voice sounded strange and thin to him, and he wished with all his heart for Marlana or Lady No, or even for Landro, to appear and discipline these murdering, rebellious soldiers.

For a moment the troopers hesitated, remembering now, when it was too late, that the penalty for mutiny and treason was a long and painful death.

The officer snapped out, "Take him. *Now.*"

And the son of Glamiss Magnifico, symbol of the Vykan Dynasty, changed from prince to prisoner in that moment.

Marlana's rooms lay on the third terrace of the citadel, a suite set far back amid gardens planted on the roofs of the second-story guardrooms and armories.

Kier waited, hands bound, between two Vegan Imperials armed with short swords. Landro was taking no chances with The Rebel, the Rhad thought ruefully.

He could see the rain falling steadily beyond the heavy, crude glass panes. The trees and shrubs in the gardens looked black-dark in the dusk. The season on Earth was spring, but the days were still short, and the weather tinged the last of the day with a bluish, mournful light. Within the hour darkness would fall. Kier thought of his cousin and murmured a silent prayer: *God be with him, and may his skill be every-*

thing it should be. To handle a great starship so delicately in the atmosphere would require the precision of an almost magical touch. Kier, religious in his way, prayed for the intercession of his dead kinsman, the beatified Emeric. Rhada and perhaps the Empire rode with Kalin's skill as a Navigator now.

Kier heard a flurry of activity in the gallery, and Landro stepped into the room. He still wore court dress, with his long hair clubbed and caught in a silver clasp. But he carried a battle sword now, naked in his hand. Kier wondered if this were the end of it—a swift thrust, and then the great mystery of death. Landro read his thoughts and showed his teeth in a smile. "Not yet, cousin. Have no fear."

The Rhad met his eyes steadily. Landro pointed to a chair with his blade and said, "Rest. You've had a tiring time."

Kier measured the distance between them. He could not reach him before the Vegans cut him down, nor were his clubbed fists enough against Landro's sword. He walked instead to the chair and sat, regarding his enemy with unveiled contempt.

Landro dismissed the troopers and stood looking at Kier speculatively.

"You surprise me," he said finally. "I did not really imagine you would come here like a steer to the slaughter."

"It's to be slaughter, then," Kier said quietly.

Landro arched his eyebrows. "Very likely, cousin."

Kier remained silent and thought of Sarissa. They were gathering there now, the star kings of the Rim worlds. Soon they would send an emissary to Earth, and when they learned of treason and usurpation, no power in the galaxy could stop the armies that would fall on Nyor. But after that would come the quarreling among the captains and the warleaders and the petty kings—and the Black Age would return. This time, perhaps forever.

The door opened and Marlana entered. She no longer wore Vykan yellow. Her dress was scarlet, the state color of hereditary kingship.

At twenty-three, Marlana of Vyka was reputed to be one of the most beautiful women in the Empire— and one of the most ambitious. Daughter of a collateral branch of the royal Vyks, she had been married to Torquas by The Magnifico himself, who had once told Kier's father, "I cannot kill her, so I must breed her to my son to heal old wounds." The old wounds were the deaths of members of her family who had tried more than once to enforce their claims to the ancient throne of the Vykan kings.

The business of kingship was a harsh one, Kier thought. Unity and Empire were often bought only at the price of the blood of kinsmen. Perhaps it had always been so. Cavour, who studied the ancient writings, said it had been since the dawn of man. The death of a royal few brought peace to the worlds sometimes. But not now, Kier thought bitterly. Not this time. If Torquas and his sister were dead, the Vykan Dynasty would fall in a rain of blood, a terror to last a thousand years.

Marlana faced the two men unsmilingly. She said to Landro, "Well?"

Landro shook his head. "I have not asked him."

Kier looked from one to the other and waited.

"Why did you come, Kier?" Marlana asked bluntly.

"I was summoned by the Galacton. Why else should I have come?"

"You can't be such a fool."

"Loyalty blinds him," Landro said ironically.

"Are you loyal?" Marlana asked.

"To the Galacton," Kier said. "The Rhad have always been."

Marlana made a cold and imperious gesture. "To the dynasty."

"Do you want me to beg for my life, Marlana?" Kier asked, controlling his growing anger.

Marlana spoke to Landro. "Show him the instrument."

Landro held a parchment before Kier's eyes. It was the Instrument of Abdication signed "Torquas Primus."

Kier remained silent.

Marlana said, "Well, Rebel?"

"The boy would sign anything you ask," Kier said. "Does that make you Queen-Empress?"

"It takes care of legalities," Landro murmured.

"It's a death warrant for Nyor," Kier said, rising to face the warleader.

Marlana glanced significantly at Landro. "What are you saying, Kier?"

The Rhad cursed his own quick anger that would make him betray Sarissa and the rebellion forming there.

"Torquas is dead, cousin," Landro said smoothly. "Marlana is twice over Queen-Empress—as successor named in this paper and as heiress to the Galacton."

Kier thought about the twelve-year-old son of his one-time general and sovereign. By all that was holy among the stars, a child should never have been made king, but there had been no better way at the time. He said a prayer for the soul of Torquas. He had no reason to doubt that Marlana and Landro would have him killed.

"If what you say is so," he said, "then Ariane is

Queen-Empress—not Marlana. She is the heiress to Glamiss and Vyka and all the worlds. We fought to make it so."

Landro said, "Ah, yes. At Karma. You were a favorite of The Magnifico's. It will pain his spirit, wherever it is, to see you die."

Marlana said, "Who speaks of dying?" She regarded Landro with calm tolerance. "You men would settle everything with killing. That is not the way of it now. Nor shall it be. I've no use for dead men. They cannot speak and they cannot serve."

But there was a cutting edge veiled under her fair words, Kier thought. With Marlana as Queen-Empress, the star kings would trade domination by the mailed fist for the greater tyranny of the cat's claws.

"You said 'a death warrant for Nyor,' Rebel," Marlana said. "What do you mean by that?"

Kier shook his head.

"The Questioner, Queen?" Landro asked, giggling eagerly.

"Not yet." Marlana's eyes rested speculatively on the Rhadan. "But we *will* know, Rebel. One way or another."

Kier thought of the kings on Tallan's world. He had imagined that he might bring them to their senses with assurances of redress from The Magnifico's son. Now that hope was dead with the boy. What remained was tyranny on the one hand, bloody war on the other. And torture for himself if he remained silent. A bitter choice for a star-voyaging warman.

"The Empire could not be ruled by a child," Marlana said, guessing his thoughts.

"It could have been," Kier said, "by a boy well served." He regarded Landro contemptuously. "Well served by honest men."

Marlana smiled. "You are an idealist then, Rebel. No, the troops are loyal to me."

"You've bought them, Marlana. But when did bought men ever stay bought? And what do you have, really? The Vegans."

"Tell me what you meant, Rebel, when you spoke of a death warrant for Nyor."

"The dynasty was new, Marlana, and Torquas too young to rule unless he was well served. But it was the only way we knew to try to keep the peace— You have destroyed all that with your bedroom rebellion. You may have me, but what of all the others? The Centauri, the Lyri, the men of Kalgan and Aldebaran and Deneb and Altair and a hundred other systems? What good will your fifty thousand Vegans be against them?"

Marlana said, "Say more, Rebel."

"No more. It's done now. Everything we fought for at Karma and a dozen other places is finished."

Marlana moved closer to Kier. He thought: *She is beautiful, the way a tree of ice is beautiful. Intelligent, ambitious, cruel. To have married her to a boy was The Magnifico's disastrous mistake, the act that would bring the young Empire crashing down.*

She said, "You have fifteen starships, Kier. And twenty thousand warmen—Rhadans, the best in the Empire. Give them to me. Serve the Empire as you always have. I do not want to destroy the Rim worlds, but if I must, I will. You could prevent it, Kier of Rhada."

Kier smiled bleakly. Marlana's ambition was royal enough. But war would not start on the Rim. It would begin here, on Earth, as the disaffected star kings blackened the capital with fire and sword. And the Rhad would be among them, led by Willim of As-

traris, burning and killing to avenge their warleader
Kier—dead in the hands of Marlana's Questioner.
That, he thought resignedly, was the way it would be.
The Rhad were a melancholy race, and Kier felt the
weight of the dour centuries in his heart, so it jarred
him to hear Marlana's laughter.

"Oh, you out-worlders," she said. "What an ancient breed you are! Glamiss used to say, 'The Rhad
see doom beyond every hill.' Is it because you live
so far away, Rebel? Out on the edge of the sky where
there are no stars to see in the night? Where is your
ambition, you brave captain? I'm offering you the
Inner Worlds if you are man enough to take them!"

"You mean treacherous enough," Kier said.

Now Landro laughed. "You see, Queen? He fought
at Karma, and he still dreams of his great king. There's
only one way with the Rhad."

Marlana turned for a moment to look through the
window at the night falling over the city of Nyor.
"Glamiss is dead, Kier. The times are changing. Will
you speak?"

Kier shook his head.

"I have sent the Vykan guard across the river into
Jersey. There are no Floridans in the tower. The city
is in the hands of the Veg. In the morning we will
take your starship. What choice have you, Rebel?"

Kier thought of Kalin and breathed a silent prayer
to the beatified Emeric.

Marlana turned and looked coldly at him. "One last
time, Kier. Think carefully."

"You will never hold what you have stolen, Marlana. This I know," Kier said.

She turned away angrily, her patience at an end.
She snapped out a command, and four Vegan Imperials stepped into the room and saluted her. "Take him

to the Questioner," she said.

The guards moved Kier to the door. Marlana said, "Good-by, Rebel. We won't meet again."

When they had gone, Marlana turned to Landro. "Find out what he knows of Sarissa."

"What can he know?"

Marlana said impatiently, "The issue is still in doubt there."

"You don't trust the cyborg?"

Marlana's eyes narrowed as she regarded the Vegan. "Far more than I'd trust any man," she said.

Landro inclined his head. There was a touch of mockery in his manner. "Then, Queen, you will be interested in my latest news."

"You've had word from Sarissa? Why wasn't I told at once?" Her lovely face was set in anger.

"There was no time. Until now, Queen."

"What is it, then?"

"It's Kelber," said Landro, smirking foolishly.

Marlana waited, reining her impatience and anger. In time, Landro would have to be taught a lesson. When all this was done, her lover would have outlived his usefulness.

"A Sarissan starship landed in Connecticut late this afternoon. A courier arrived only an hour ago."

"From the cyborg?"

"Please. From the Sarissan star king," Landro said. "It seems that there has been a fire in the city of Sardis. The entire Street of Night was destroyed."

"And Kelber?"

"Dead, Queen."

Marlana walked swiftly to the window and stood in thoughtful silence. Full night had fallen over Nyor. The torchlights of the watch flickered in the rainy darkness. "You think the cyborg killed him," she said finally.

"Who can say, Queen?"

Marlana turned, a decision made. "All right. You leave for Sarissa tonight. Within the hour. Tallan can't be left alone."

"As you command, love," Landro said.

"Why do you look like that?" Marlana asked irritably.

"I was only thinking that before you learned of Kelber's death, you spoke of 'the cyborg.' But now that you suspect an act of murder, it's become 'Tallan,' as though he were a man." Landro fidgeted nervously with the silver clasps in his hair and asked in an arch voice, "So who can you trust now, my queen?"

Chapter Seven

The maneuvering of starships at low speeds and in atmosphere requires the coordinated efforts of a control team specially trained in Ionics, Planetary Magnetic Effects, and Pilotage. In the absence of such rated personnel, close maneuvering at low levels should not be attempted.

Golden Age fragment found
at Station One, Astraris

To study, to learn, to safeguard that which is holy, and above all, to dare: that is the duty of a Navigator.

Attributed to Emeric of Rhada,
Grand Master of Navigators,
early Second Stellar Empire period

KALIN, the Navigator, stood in the entry valve of the Rhadan starship and watched the swift and orderly withdrawal of the last warmen of the perimeter guard. As the horses padded aboard, he could hear them complaining at a new confinement. They were restless because there had been no battle with their armored cousins of Vega.

The arbalests had been stowed, and Nevus paced the landing ground, urging the warmen to greater speed and more silence. Through the rainy darkness Kalin could see the cooking fires of the Imperials and, beyond that, barely visible in the gloomy night, the few torchlights of Nyor.

The young priest-Navigator stood tensely, waiting moment by moment for the alarm that must surely come from the Imperial pickets when they discovered the swift and secret withdrawal of the Rhadans. But there was no sound but the soft padding of the disgruntled war horses and an occasional soft chink of iron as a weapon touched against harness. The rain and the darkness were covering the maneuver perfectly, as Kier had foreseen that they would.

The last troopers filed through into the interior of the starship, and Kalin rubbed his sweating palms against the coarse cloth of his robe. Underneath he could feel the unyielding scales of god-metal that protected him from neck to thigh.

Now Nevus stepped through the valve and stood for a moment looking back at the darkness where the Imperials rested around their fires.

"Well, it worked the way he said it would," the old warrior said, "At least so far. Is it time, priest?"

"As nearly as can be figured without the stars to see," Kalin said.

Nevus regarded him unsmilingly but not unkindly. "Anxious, boy?"

Kalin was about to reply with some unctuous remark from the dogma but thought better of it. "Yes," he said. "I don't know if I am good enough, General."

"He thinks you are," Nevus replied. "The Rhad don't fail."

Kalin nodded, lips compressed. He was thinking of the darkness and the search through the rainy air for the spire. But the ship's own glow would give some light. His mind abandoned anxiety, and he concerned himself with the technical problems of pilotage involved. He drew a deep breath and tried to look soldierly. *If Kier thinks I can do it,* he thought, *then I must.* "We will start now," he said.

Kalin entered the sacred part of the starship, stepped swiftly over the coaming into the control room, and made a perfunctory sign of the Star in the air. The two novices already at their posts before the banks of ancient instrument panels looked up, acknowledged the priest-Navigator's blessing, and stood by for orders.

Their faces were pale under the cowls. Kalin felt a sudden decisive confidence invade his spirit. He wondered briefly if it was the shade of his beatified ancestor Emeric coming to aid him in his moment of trial. If so, he was well served. It was said that no finer pilot of starships had ever lived than Emeric of Rhada.

"Brother John," Kalin said. "Close the valve."

"Yes, First Pilot," the novice replied respectfully, using the holy title that was never used in the hearing of unconsecrated persons.

"Brother Yakob, start the power sequence."

The two novices, their confidence increased by having something familiar and important to do, bent to their Sacred tasks.

In this holiest part of the ship, the mysterious force "electricity" still lived. Kalin took his position in the

pilot's couch and touched the switches that activated
the transparent cone covering the control room. As
his hands moved in the prescribed passes over the
panel, he automatically recited the appropriate pray-
ers. "Great is the power of Almighty God who lives
between the stars and gives us the power to see." The
walls seemed to dissolve, and the control room became an island floating in space above the rubbled
landing ground at the south end of the great Tel-
Manhat. Through the rain, in the middle distance,
Kalin could see the shadowy shapes of the Imperials
moving across the fires. The ground around the ship
reflected a growing radiance as the power sequence
progressed, and surely now the Vegans were discov-
ering that the starship was preparing to depart.

"Energy Level One, blessed be the Name," Brother
Yakob intoned.

"Starship in all respects ready for flight, First Pilot,"
Brother John reported.

"Energy Two," Kalin ordered.

"Energy Two sequence begun," Brother Yakob said.

The light around the ship grew brighter, the air
ionizing so that the falling raindrops seemed bits of
molten violet. Through the aurora Kalin could see
signal torches being waved in the Imperial ranks. Already a squadron of mounted Vegans was plunging
across the uneven ground toward the starship, but they
could only mill about in mingled anger and fear, for
the ship was sealed and no power their world knew
could open it.

"Energy Two, First Pilot," said Brother Yakob.

"Maneuver sequence, hallowed be the Spirit," Kalin
commanded.

"Begun, for the glory of the Lord," Brother John
responded.

Kalin could feel the great starship coming to life beneath him, all around him. For the young priest, this was the holiest and most exalting of moments, as the eternal power of the most sacred objects in the universe responded to his touch. There was an ancient prayer, a fragment of one of the holiest books preserved by the order, that Kalin always spoke silently at such a moment: a private devotion, not prescribed by the dogma, but a beautiful phrase that must surely have been recorded by the Dawn Men for the instant when flight began. Kalin closed his eyes and said inaudibly, "Arise my love, arise and come away with me—" The starship's immense weight rode the planet's magnetic lines of force and lifted from the depression it had made in the earth of the tel. It seemed to float on the radiance of the wet, shining air.

Only meters below the massive curve of the keel, the now thoroughly aroused Imperials milled in angry frustration. One or two of the more daring launched throwing spears and an occasional arrow at the rising colossus, but these were impious acts and the missiles fell back uselessly. Some of the troopers retreated from them in superstitious dread of the radiance that clung to them for a time only to fade as the vessel rose higher still into the rainy night.

The starship floated upward above the upturned faces of the Imperial officers who now were terrified of the report they must give to the warleader Landro. The glow of ionization grew dimmer as the ship's altitude increased. At some six hundred meters the great ship reached the cloud layer, and now those below could only see a faint violet light moving within the low mists. But the radiance did not fade away to nothing as the ship reached for space. Instead, it lingered above the tel, hovering within the cloud, fading for moments at a time as the rain fell harder, then reappearing as the wind opened patches of darkness in the air.

Then slowly, almost imperceptibly, the light moved northward toward the city.

Chapter Eight

During the political convulsions that shook the capital during the uprisings of the early Second Stellar Empire period, one loyalty remained unquestioned. This was the devotion of the Vykan soldiery to the persons of the royal family.

Nv. Julianus Mullerium, *The Age of the Star Kings*,
middle Second Steller Empire period

Fear the Vulk, for he sees without eyes and knows the black arts and dreams of the blood of children. He is not as men. He is without loyalty.

Preface to *The Vulk Protocols*,
authorship unknown,
Interregnal period

THE Vulk known to humans by the name of Erit stood rigidly against the stones of the spiraling passageway cut into the citadel wall. All around her in the darkness, the Vykan warmen waited for her to waken from her dream. She was conscious of them, conscious of the slender girl in mail war-harness kneeling at her side, but their nearness was only a distraction, and Erit forced the luminous images out of her mind and reached into the night.

A tremor shook her slight form as the contact grew stronger. So near. So very near. It had been a very long time since Erit had touched one of her own, and it would have given her great pleasure, but there was death and danger in the air, in the night, everywhere.

> *Where?*
> *Near, sister. Very near. Above you.*
> *A thousand greetings. Peace.*
> Impatience. *You are young, sister. There is no peace.*
> *We will come to you.*
> *Can you?*
> *We must. We are in a trap.*
> *No more than we.*
> *But you hope. I can hear it.*
> *Forgive me. I should have known she was with you.*

The warmen muttered in the darkness. There were only five. The sixth had died in the tower room. But there were nine dead Vegans there. The youngest soldier, fresh this last month from Vyka, thought about the mountains and lakes of his home world and wondered bleakly if he would ever see his land again. Then he glanced uneasily at the trance-held Vulk and wondered if it could truly read his thoughts as people said. He squared his shoulders and rubbed the thin sword cut on his arm. It didn't matter if the Vulk could, though it would be unfitting if the creature should tell the princess of his feelings. He swallowed hard and moved closer to Ariane. He would give his life for her, and he very nearly had when his detachment had sneaked back into the city from across the river to attack the Vegans guarding her. He stole a glance at the face hidden under the cap of god-metal and thought, with all the sincerity of his eighteen years: *I shall defend her with my last breath*. Then he thought sadly that in a palace now suddenly filled with mutinous Imperials, it seemed likely that he would soon be called upon to fulfill that promise.

Ariane said, "Erit, can you hear me?"

The Vulk did not reply. Her hands clenched and opened with the effort to maintain contact.

Do you see what is around me? Do you know where we are?

Erit trembled with eagerness. *Yes. Now I see. You are in the tower.*

Can you bring her here?

She will seek your— The idea was a Vulk concept for which there was no human counterpart. It contained elements of brotherhood, devotion, kinship, almost symbiosis. It was to the other Vulk what Ariane was to Erit—that human person without which no Vulk could be complete.

Excitement. Hope.

Find him! He is in pain. I can feel it.

It will endanger her. The ancient Vulk conflict now: one trapped into opposition with another because their human symbiotes' interests might clash.

Erit felt an overpowering command. The Vulk Gret was far older and more nearly mature than she. Her mind wavered under the power of his authority. Erit shivered and withdrew. She sank to the cold stone ramp, trembling and exhausted.

Ariane cradled Erit in her arms. Presently, the Vulk murmured, "Rhadans. In the tower. Somehow they think they can escape—"

"Kier's men. Gret."

"Yes, Ariane. Gret." Erit shivered again as she said the name. "They said to come, if we can."

"And Kier?"

The Vulk remained silent.

"Gret must know where he is. He has been with him since childhood."

"As I have with you, Ariane."

Ariane's anger flashed suddenly. "Where is he? I command you, Erit. Speak or I send you from me!"

Erit did not reply that in their present circumstances— or for that matter, in any others—what Ariane threatened was impossible for them both. She shrugged her thin shoulders in a Vulk gesture of resignation. If Ariane died, then Erit would die as well. So in the cosmic eternity, what did it matter?

"He is with the Questioner," the Vulk said.

The question room lay deep in the tel under the Citadel. To reach it meant a journey along passageways that had once, long ago, been lined with rails of god-metal. No one knew how long ago these tunnels through Tel-Manhat had been built nor for what purpose. In most places the ancient rails had rusted away, and in others the metal had been removed to be resmelted into armor and weapons.

Kier had tried to remember the route the squad of Imperials had taken, but he was unaccustomed to these underground warrens, and by the time he had been delivered to the black-garbed executioners who served the Questioner, he was thoroughly lost. His Rhadan courage sustained him, but his Rhadan melancholy prepared him for a lingering and painful death.

At the moment he was thinking of Gret. The contact was very strong. Gret was still alive and filled with strange Vulk excitements, perhaps caused by the nearness of freedom. It would be almost time for the starship to appear.

The Questioner was a large masked man in black. The post was traditionally anonymous to safeguard the person of the state torturer from the vengeance of his many victims' relations and dependents. And the man's very anonymity surrounded him and his domain with dread.

The Imperials had stationed themselves outside the torchlit room, and the executioners, seven of them by tradition and law, had delivered the young Rhad to their master in silence.

In the question room all commands were given by signal, and only the Questioner himself spoke to the detainee.

The huge, black-clad man had a surprisingly high-pitched and effeminate voice that heightened the feeling of increasing horror.

"A Rhadan star king, no less." The lips that showed through the opening in the sable mask were red and shining. The teeth were long and white, like flat slabs of porcelain. "What will they send me next, I wonder?"

He signaled to his helpers. They crowded around Kier like demons. He could sense their eagerness for the questioning to begin.

"Now, my pretties," the Questioner said. "We cannot begin this minute. We have to know what questions to ask, don't we? But we *can* prepare, yes. By all the cybs and little demons, we *can* do that."

His movements were graceful for so large a man. He walked around the chamber lightly, examining his devices. The hands on Kier's flesh felt cold and dry, like the hands of corpses.

The room had a concrete floor and white tiled walls.

The railed tunnel extended through one side of the chamber, and heavy wooden doors had been built where the roadbed entered and left the open area. That part of the room had been planked over to the level of the floor, and the remainder of the chamber contained a devilish assortment of god-metal and wooden machines intended to stretch, break, and twist the human body.

"What shall it be?" the Questioner murmured happily. "Not the rack. No, not the rack for a star king. Too common, a death without style." He turned toward a dark brazier containing rods and pincers. "The fire? How would the fire suit you, King?"

Kier regarded him coldly and hoped that the dread in his heart did not show. A stinking way for a warman to die; under torture in a hole in the earth half the sky away from his own lands.

"The Queen," the Questioner said. "Yes, I think so. For a star king—the Queen."

Kier followed him with his eyes as he walked to a statue of god-metal formed in the likeness of a woman with extended arms. The metal face was serene, the standing pose voluptuous.

The red lips smiled, and the eyes behind the mask glittered. "Look at our beautiful lady, King. See how she waits to embrace you." He giggled grotesquely. "I hear that the royal Rhad are great lovers of women. What could be more fitting than a tryst with the Queen of the question room?"

Kier studied the metal woman and saw that the arms were hinged at the shoulders. From the back of the statue projected a screw device, like the twist handle of a great wine press. A shudder of horror passed through him.

The Questioner signaled his helpers, and they pulled

Kier across the room until he stood facing the metal woman. They raised his bound wrists and forced them over the head of the statue so that he hung helplessly against the cold body.

"Now gently, gently," the Questioner said. "Let her embrace him."

An executioner began to turn the screw, and Kier felt the unyielding touch of the arms closing about him. It took all of his will not to struggle, not to give his torturers the satisfaction of seeing a Rhadan warman flinch from what must come.

The arms closed more tightly about him, crushing him against the metal breasts, driving the breath from him. A cold sweat broke out on his face, and tiny lancets of pain shot through his chest. The Questioner was studying his face with the interest of an expert, gauging his pain. He signaled a quarter turn on the screw and smiled in satisfaction as the metal arms sent a streak of agony through Kier.

"Ah, there. We'll leave him so for a time." The heavy black figure shook with enjoyment. "Let him become accustomed to his Queen. Too much love is a bad thing, even for a mighty Rhad."

There was a hollow roaring in Kier's head. His compressed lungs struggled to breathe. A darkness flickered before his eyes, and he wondered how long his superbly conditioned body would betray him by staying alive and in such pain.

He imagined he could hear the sound of clashing weapons beyond the wooden door to the question room, but he was certain he must be mistaken. Perhaps it was only the iron sound of the gears inside the Queen.

The executioners had left him. He could not turn his head to see what was happening, but one moved by him holding a weapon. There was a crashing of bodies against the door and then the noise of combat inside the question room. Kier strained to free himself from the machine's embrace, feeling blood flow down his side as his own mail tore his flesh.

The Questioner gave a womanish cry of mingled fear and anger, and suddenly he was at the screw, throwing his weight against it with that desperation of executioners—that vindictive rage that demands a victim should die rather than be set free.

The Queen's arms tightened. Kier knew that in another moment his chest would be crushed. Two warmen, Vyks by their harness, appeared in the torch-light. Behind them one of the Questioner's helpers staggered against the wall, his black clothing stained with red.

A warman pulled the Questioner away from the Queen, and the other, with a quick motion, passed a blade in and out of the fat body. Kier did not see him fall. For the young star king there was only pain and darkness.

Chapter Nine

Hee tooke a course, which since, successfully/ Great men have often taken, to espie/ The counsels, or to breake the plots of foes.

Attributed to John Donne (or Dunne), poet-religious of the pre-Golden Age period. Fragment found at Biblios Brittanis, Mars

Men called her Princess
Men called her Queen
Wore she armor of purest gold
And loved she well her Rim-world king
She whom the warmen called—Ariane!

Guest Song, authorship unknown, early Second Stellar Empire period

"HE will live, Ariane," the Vulk Erit said.

Kier opened his eyes and drew breath after breath into his aching lungs. He could see Vyk warmen standing over him; his head rested on someone's mailed thighs, and a Vulk's hands massaged the bruised muscles of his chest.

He looked up to see who was caring for him so gently. The girl dressed in Vykan war harness was young and very beautiful. Her hair was dark and cropped so that it formed a dark crown around the clear-featured face. The eyes were dark blue and slightly tilted.

He half smiled and said, "Is this the crystal starship, then? I'm on my way to paradise?"

"Kier of Rhada," the girl said with mingled anger and relief, "how could you have walked into Marlana's trap without a thought?"

Kier sat up carefully, testing his battered body. The Vulk had done well with him.

He looked long and silently at the girl. "It's Ariane, isn't it? I remember you."

The blue eyes flashed with swift anger. "Should I be complimented, Rhad? You didn't answer my question. How could you have been such a fool?"

Kier flexed his arms, wincing at the pain. "I suspected misfeasance, not treason"—he frowned and his face grew dark—"and murder."

Ariane's shoulders sagged under the mail. "Is it true, then? They have killed my brother?"

Kier's voice was low. "They say so, Queen."

At his use of the title, the Vykans murmured among themselves and looked at Ariane with a new, almost fearful expression.

Kier stood unsteadily and rested his weight against the dark figure of the god-metal woman whose embrace had almost been his undoing. Then he took Ariane's hands and pulled her gently to her feet. Her eyes were shining with sudden tears, but he pretended not to notice them. He swept the room with a glance.

The Questioner and his men lay still on the concrete floor. The Vykans stood uncertainly. Kier spoke directly to them. "How many more of you are there still here?"

A young warman, a boy of eighteen, not more, said, "Only what you see, King. They ordered the whole division of us across the river into camp. When we got there, five hundred Imperials were there with missile weapons to watch us."

"But you five came back."

"There were six of us. Our sergeant died when we fought the Veg guarding Ariane. There were nine of them," he added with a touch of pride, "and they are all dead." He paused uncertainly, not knowing how exactly to speak to a Rhad captain without sounding boastful. "The six of us, King," he added, "are from Vyka. From Ariane's lands."

Kier looked thoughtfully at the girl. He said, almost with sadness, for he knew what he must put upon her, "From the Queen's lands."

A transformation took place in the boy's face. Ariane, a great noble, had, with Kier's words, soared even higher—near to divinity in the simple warman's world. He dropped to his knees, murmuring, "Empress," and the others did the same.

Ariane said quickly, "We cannot be sure my brother is dead, Kier." She looked at the Rhad appealingly, but he could offer her no escape. He would need her now—and henceforward. Political reality would not spare her.

He touched his knee to the ground and said formally, "The Rhad are your soldiers, Queen-Empress."

Her protest died without words. Presently, she replied in the words of the ancient Vyk ritual, "If the King be truly dead, the Queen rules."

Kier stood immediately and turned to the warmen. A hard smile touched his lips. "This isn't much for an Imperial army, but it must serve for now." He addressed the Vulk. "I know you, Erit."

"I know you, King."

"Touch Gret," he commanded.

"I have, King."

"He is in the tower?"

"He is."

Kier nodded grimly. "One thing has gone right, at least."

Kier walked, controlling his pain, to the dead Questioner and took his sword. "Ariane," he said sharply, "have all the Imperials mutinied?"

The girl regarded him tight-lipped for a moment before replying. "All the Vegans."

"The Floridans in the tower?"

"I don't know."

"Erit?"

The Vulk shrugged. "Gret could sense only Vegans, King."

"Can you reach him now?"

"No, King. I have not the strength so soon again."

Kier addressed the young Vyk. "Can one of you guide us to the tower?"

"Not through the tel, King. We don't know the way."

"Ariane?"

The girl shook her head.

"Then it will have to be above ground. Is it still raining?"

"Yes, King," a Vykan said.

"Thank God for that." He looked once again about the torchlit question room and thought: I owe you for this, Landro. "We go, then."

"To the tower?" the young Vyk objected. "Why not across the river?"

"Let the Vykans rest there for a time. We may have need of them later." He spoke in the tone of a man accustomed to commanding, and the warmen were quick to acknowledge it.

Ariane, however, spoke angrily. "You made me Queen-Empress, Rhad. Are you God that we must all obey you?"

Kier suppressed admiring laughter. She was truly The Magnifico's daughter. "Forgive me, Queen. But until you have an army of more than six men and a Vulk, I'll have to ask that you follow me."

The girl looked at him, blue eyes sparking. "So be it, Rebel. You are my warleader."

Kier retrieved Ariane's helmet. "Please cover your face, Queen-Empress." The girl was too great a prize to risk recognition if they should have to fight their way to the Empire Tower.

She took the metal cap and put it on her head. "Until I have an army greater than a Vulk, five Vykans, and one arrogant Rhad, you may call me Ariane," she said.

Kier half smiled. "And afterward?"

"We will see," she answered pridefully. "I may have your head on a lance."

With five hundred Imperials watching the Vyk division on the Jersey shore, a thousand more deployed at the landing ground, and most of the remainder concentrated at the citadel, the city of Nyor was thinly garrisoned. Kier gave thanks for that. With the young Vyk in the lead, the small band made its way cautiously through the dark streets, hiding from the watch.

Kier searched the sky for the telltale glow of the

starship, but the rain clouds lay low and heavy over
the city, and he could see nothing. The rain sluiced
down, and now a wind had risen. Kier wondered if
the rain was really poisoned on Earth as the legends
said. It was one of those tales found in the *Book of
Warls*. Perhaps it had once been true. "The rain brings
death," the *Warls* said, "from the burning of a thousand suns." To Kier, however, much more worrisome
was the rising wind. A starship in hovering flight was
nearly weightless, and a gusting, stormy wind could
make Kalin's task almost impossible.

They walked on ground like that of Schliemann's
Troy, though they would not have known either name.
In the dawn of their time, New York had been reduced
to rubble a hundred times; reduced and rebuilt again.
Each age had left its detritus, layer on layer to form
the gigantic island mound now known as Tel-Manhat
and the primitive city that ruled the stars—the city
of Nyor.

In single file, and watchfully, they traveled the
narrow avenue down the length of the tel toward the
Empire Tower. Twice they hid in dark doorways and
alleys to evade the watch, nervously patrolling the
city on this rainy night that seemed filled with unease
for all the Nyori.

The people remained indoors, gathered around lan-
terns and tallow candles, while those who had been
there to see the Rhadan star king ride so foolishly
gallant into the citadel told of what they had seen and
what they feared would come. The Nyori were a people made cynical by history. They guarded themselves
and no others.

"The Vyks have been ordered out of the city," a
sharp-eyed grandfather would say.

"The Imperials will kill them all," a child might add, with the blood-thirst of innocence.

"And the Rhad. What of him?"

"Aiee, he will not come out of the citadel again."

"A pity. He was a brave warleader."

"But too trusting for the Inner Worlds. Too simple for Nyor." And with that, the old one would end the talk, and the family would wait to see what the morning might bring.

The Vulk Erit stumbled in the wet darkness. Kier motioned to a warman. "Carry her."

The warman, repressing a shudder out of loyalty to Ariane, swept the Vulk onto his shoulders.

Erit said, "The tower is nearby. Half a kilometer. Less."

None of the party could see the looming mass in the rainy dark—only the eyeless Vulk.

Kier slowed to walk with Ariane. "I am sorry about Torquas, Queen," he said in a low voice.

"If they have truly killed him, Kier," the girl said steadily, "I'll have their hearts roasted."

Kier's smile was hidden by the shadows. "You shall have them, God willing."

"But he was only a boy, Kier—" It seemed for a moment that her voice would break. Kier would not have that—not here and now.

"He was Galacton and The Magnifico's son, Ariane."

The girl looked at him, and in a stray beam of light from a window he could see her eyes glittering—whether with tears or anger he could not tell.

"Twelve years old." She accented the words bitterly.

"And a king. *The* King."

Ariane shook her head. "What savages we are, Kier. Is there no other way to rule?"

Kier, his feudal mind coldly fixed on what must be done, said harshly, "I know of none."

The girl would have replied, but the Vykan in the lead stopped abruptly and held up his hand for silence. Kier hurried to his side.

"There," the Vyk said. "A guard on the tower gate."

In the light of a torch sputtering in the rain, four Vegans lounged in the mouth of the archway opening into the tower.

Kier signaled the Vyk carrying Erit forward. The man put the Vulk down with relief. Kier said, "Are you rested, Vulk?"

"Some, King."

"Four we can see. How many more can you sense?"

The smoothly contoured face lifted toward the façade of the immense and ancient building.

"On this level only those four. Five stories above a guardroom—with many. More than ten. I cannot sense them clearly."

Kier knelt so that his face was level with the Vulk's. He put his hands on her shoulders. "Sense me, Erit. What do you see?"

The Vulk shivered. "You are angry."

"Yes, yes," Kier said impatiently. "What else?"

"You want to fight—to kill—to—" The small creature began to tremble violently. "You are still in pain, King."

"Am I strong enough to lead? Or must another do it?"

"You are strong enough."

A grim smile touched Kier's lips. "Can you reach Gret now?"

"I will try, King."

Kier waited while the Vulk grew tense and rigid with effort. In Erit's unhuman mind, the pictures formed fleetingly. *Gret. Brother.* She felt him somewhere in the vast darkness above her.

Sister! Here! A command.

She struggled to hold the mind-contact.

He is with you. It was not a question. Gret knew.

Yes.

"How many guard them?" Kier demanded.

Vegans. Many. A light in the mists above— The contact faded. One lingering touch that cried out: *Hurry!*

Erit's delicate shoulders sagged under Kier's hands, and he was moved by her gift. Kier knew that Vulks could be rendered empty by the strain of prolonged mind-contact.

He gathered up the bird-light creature and carried her to Ariane. The girl took her and said in an angry, low voice, "And have you drained her, Rebel?"

"No, Queen," he said shortly. He turned away and gathered the Vyks about him, speaking in low tones.

Presently, two warmen melted into the shadows to the left and two more to the right. Kier slipped his sword down the back of his mailed shirt so that his head hid the projecting hilt. To the last Vyk he gave orders to stay with Ariane and Erit.

"I'm not to fight for my own, then?" Ariane demanded in an imperious whisper.

"Not yet, Queen," Kier said. "Your warleader will tell you when."

Before she could reply to that, he walked into the cobbled street toward the pool of light and the guards. He walked unsteadily and began to sing a Vegan barracks song in a muddled voice.

The Veg stood to watch him. Two of them strung

their crossbows. The officer stepped forward and challenged him.

"You there. What do you want here at this time of night?"

Kier raised an arm in a Veg salute and said muzzily, "Comrades! Take me in out of this poisonous rain, won't you?"

"This is a forbidden area," the officer said sharply. "Get out."

"A drink, for the love of the Star," Kier said.

The two crossbowmen took aim, and Kier yelled in mock alarm, raising his hands to his head. The officer stepped closer. Kier's fingers touched the hilt of the sword behind his head.

"Now!" he cried, and the blade was in his hand. There were two swift flashes, and the crossbowmen fell with thrown swords piercing their mailed shirts. The officer gave a yell of alarm and drew. Kier's blade moved with deadly swiftness, and within seconds the man was rolling onto his face on the wet cobblestones.

The fourth Veg had broken for the inside of the tower only to be met by the naked blades of two Vyks. Kier gave a sharp command not to kill him. He signaled Ariane and the remaining Vyk to come across the street.

When they had gathered in the darkness of the archway, Kier put his point to the terrified Vegan's throat and said, "How many more of you in the guardroom?"

The man shook his head, and Kier pressed the godmetal tip harder into the flesh. "Speak, you loyal soldier," he said gently.

"Twenty," the man whispered.

"And the Floridans?"

"Below. In the tel." The frightened warman tried

to move away from the point, but his back was against
the stones. His eyes, huge with fear, rolled toward
the helmeted face of the small soldier with the awful
Vulk. He shuddered and wished he could make the
sign of the Star, but he was afraid to move lest this
wild warrior wearing the strange harness cut his throat
out.

Kier stepped back, swiftly reversed his weapon,
and knocked the man unconscious. "Tie him and gag
him. Use his harness." He laughed shortly. "Some
day the Rhad and the Vyks will make up a song about
this," he said.

Chapter Ten

"And what, then, shall we do with the warlocks who profane the ancient knowledge, Grand Master?"

"First be certain that their enquiries are truly the work of sin. Then you may ask."

Emeric of Rhada, *The Dialogues*,
early Second Stellar Empire

What is the Unholy Trinity? The warlock, the Vulk, and science.

The Vulk Protocols,
authorship unknown,
Interregnal period

CAVOUR stood at the open window, and the rising wind flared his dark cloak and ruffled his gray-black beard. He could see nothing but the glow of an occasional light from the tower itself against the storm and the rain falling like drops of molten amber.

"They are coming now," Gret said.

The warlock turned to look across the room at the pale, fragile blind face. There was a sick worry in him, and fear, too, he would admit that. But his mind was restless, and it touched a thousand things and asked a hundred unanswerable questions, for that was the nature of warlocks. This tower, who built it? And when? Was it truly the work of the Dawn Men? Why did it stand through the millennia, like a monstrous spear jammed into the heart of the mound of Tel-Manhat?

He regarded Gret narrowly. Not without liking, for the creature was worthy enough. But what was he? Where did he come from? Had there always been Vulks among men? It seemed so, yet it could not be. Only man and Vulk lived among the stars, and the Vulk clung to man with a devotion that was super-human, truly so, no matter what the fearful said.

He watched as Gret touched his lyre. The soldiers had not taken it from him. Negligence? Or design? And whose? He turned again to the window and tried to see the hidden earth far below. By the Star, what a treasure house down there, where the soil could be scratched with a dagger point and it would give up mysteries and riddles—coins, machines, carvings, fragments. *The whole history of our race is there*, the warlock thought, *if we could only read it*. He made a wry face at the darkness and amended the thought: *If we could only study it and be allowed to live. Science is sin—the black equation, the heritage of the Dark Time. How many years, centuries? More than a man could count*. He drew his damp robe about him and shivered.

"Nearer," the Vulk said dreamily, his fingers caressing the strings.

The warlock said, "But nothing out *there*."

The Vulk stopped playing. He crouched in an attitude of prayer. "At the guardroom now. Slipping past in the darkness." He murmured something in an alien tongue. The warlock wondered if he were invoking the aid of his own nonhuman gods.

"A long climb, Warlock," Gret murmured.

"Are we to do nothing to help them?" Cavour asked. He could hear the Vegans in the room outside the godmetal door. They were gaming at Stars and Comets, quarreling over their throws.

Cavour returned again to the window, searching the upper darkness. There was nothing there that he could see. But a freak of the wind cleared away the mists below, and he suddenly saw a procession of torches and men, tiny as ants in the distance, running down the crooked street toward the base of the tower. Imperials, a whole squadron of them. The wind brought the faint sound of alarms. Cavour's heart sank. It was Kier they were seeking. His escape was discovered at last. He said anxiously, "They can't go back."

The Vulk shook his head. "They never could." He rose to his feet and said, "Call the guards now. It is time."

Cavour cast one more despairing glance out of the window. "There is nothing there, Gret."

"It is time," the Vulk said, and Cavour nodded and began pounding on the metal door with his clenched fists.

The guardroom was behind and below them. They had slipped past one at a time while the secure Imperials slept or quarreled or polished their weapons. But on the floor above were others. Kier guessed as many as eight or ten. They would not have guarded a warlock and a Vulk with fewer.

He could hear the sound of music. It was Gret, of

course, playing his hypnotic airs for the warmen, distracting them from their obvious—and mutinous—duties.

Ariane said, "Have you led us into another blind alley, Rebel?"

He smiled at her temper and did not reply. His chest and arms still throbbed with the iron Queen's embrace, and there was nothing ahead but fighting and danger, but he felt a savage joy to have a weapon in his hand again and a simple job of combat to do. The complexities and politics would come later, on Sarissa, if they lived to reach that place.

Erit heard the music and murmured something in a language none could understand. The Vykans made the sign of the Star in the air and commended their souls to God. They would fight, and perhaps die, in the midst of magic they did not understand. If their Ariane and the Rhad were not afraid, then they would try to disregard their own superstitious fear. But Vulks and warlocks filled them with dread.

Kier gathered them on the narrow metal stairway. They rested themselves from the long, long climb in the narrow shaft and listened to him.

"There's no time for tricks and not much chance they would succeed anyway," he said. "Gret has their attention—some of them, at least, will be listening to him. They'll be slow to react to us. I know what Vulk music can do. Make ready now."

The warmen drew their weapons. And this time, so did Ariane. "We need every sword," she said.

Kier looked down at the clear blue eyes under the metal cap and felt his heart beat faster. By the Star, what a queen for the Rhad she would make. But he should not think of that now. She would be queen to all the worlds. That thought brought a nick of sadness.

As though she read his thought, she smiled for a moment and then grew somber. "Why do we wait, Kier?"

She might have meant one thing or another. He chose to think she meant only the first. "A moment, Queen," he murmured.

Erit raised her blind face and spoke, but not with her own voice. *"There is a light in the sky, King!"*

"Now, go!" Kier shouted, and plunged up the remaining stairs into the guardroom.

There were six Imperials in the guardroom. The door to the cell chamber stood open, and Kier could see three more of the Vegan warmen within. The place resounded with the wild twanging of Gret's song.

The first Imperial died with his sword only half drawn, so caught by the music had he been. The others took warning and formed a battle line, for they were trained troops, though softened by too long duty in the capital.

Beside Kier the Vykans were fighting, and the enclosed and badly lit rooms resounded to the ring of swords. The man opposing Kier was a good swordsman and strong. It took the young star king time to pierce his shoulder and disarm him. He made no move to prevent his bolt for the stairway leading down. There was no time to worry about that now because Kier could see through the other room to the window, where the mists seemed to glow with a dancing violet light.

Another Vegan went down, and Kier turned to face a third. Ariane stood at his side as firmly as any trooper. He felt a surge of pride for her.

Cavour had made a snare from his cloak and had caught an Imperial from behind. Gret and Erit were singing a wild, skirling melody. There was a touch of madness in the scene of dancing shadows, clashing blades, and alien music.

Then, quite suddenly, a silence fell because the last of the guards lay still on the floor. The young Vyk was wounded, cut on the neck above his mailed shirt. But he was on his feet and regarding Ariane with worshipful eyes. *We savages,* Kier thought, *how we love a warrior queen!*

Cavour, at the window now, called out to Kier, "It's there! I see it now!"

God reward Kalin, Kier thought, *and make his hand steady.* Ariane was staring, half afraid, at the ionized rain falling past the casements and on down into the abyss. "Kier—is it—?"

"My starship, Ariane. And my very skillful cousin."

No one in the Empire, Ariane thought, had ever attempted to maneuver a starship so delicately, so close to the ground. A touch could bring shattering disaster, an explosion greater than the missiles of ancient legend.

From below came the noise of armored men running. Kier ordered the Vykans to the casement. He stood there, straining his eyes against the now-brilliant mists. It seemed he could sense the immense bulk of the starship frighteningly close, but still he could not see it.

"There!" cried the young Vyk. "I see an open valve!"

Now Kier and the others could see it as well. The dilating aperture seemed a tunnel hanging in a swirling, glowing space. It bobbed and swayed grotesquely as the winds tore at the thousand-meter-long hull of the antique vessel. Across a gap of five meters Kier could see the hulking shape of his lieutenant-general Nevus and a crew of warmen with a casting line. But the noises of pursuit grew louder, mingled with the sacred humming of the starship.

The line came hurtling into the room and, without being told, the Vyks made it fast.

"Go quickly now!" Kier commanded. "Cavour, take Gret. You, warman—what's your name?"

"Han, sir," the boy said.

"Are you too hurt to cross carrying Erit?"

"I can make it, King."

"Do it then, and quickly!"

The boy looked longingly at the stairway, and Kier cursed him for a berserk Vyk who thought more of fighting than of his queen. The parade ground tongue-lashing spurred him into action, and he lifted Erit to his shoulders.

"Go now, Cavour," Kier commanded. The warlock, with Gret clinging to his neck, swung hand over hand along the wildly gyrating line. Kier saw him safely into the starship's portal and shoved the boy Han to the casement. He, too, made the hair-raising crossing.

Ariane looked at the line with a sinking heart. She knew her strength unequal to the crossing. Kier had thought of almost everything but not of that. She motioned her remaining Vyks to the window. They crossed, swinging crazily in the wind a kilometer above the city.

Kier, alone now with Ariane, unshipped the casting line and lashed it to her harness. For a moment the girl did not realize what he was doing, and when she did, she fought him with a sudden angry despair.

"I didn't set you free so you could throw your life away, Kier!"

Kier took the helmet from her head so that her dark hair blew in the wind from the window. "We are not beaten yet," he said. "But in case something goes badly—" He laughed with the pleasure of battle and kissed her. "Be a proper queen and *go!*"

He took the sword from her and shouted to Nevus and Cavour to take her. She stood for a moment on the casement, looking back at him, and then she was gone, swinging on the end of the casting line as the men in the starship hauled her into the valve.

Kier turned to face the soldiery pouring into the outer room from the stairway. He looked back to see that the open valve of the starship was still in sight, moving, in fact, closer to the building as Kalin worked his incomprehensible magic half a kilometer away in the unseen prow of the vessel.

Kier raised one of the swords and threw it like a spear at the first man to burst through the doorway. Before the man had fallen, Ariane's weapon was in his hand and flashing after his own.

Then Kier turned, ran across the room, and launched himself into space.

The rain and wind were icy on his naked skin. He seemed to be suspended in a glowing limbo where all was light and violence. His arms and hands, extended before him, gleamed with a ghost light.

Then he struck the hull of the starship, clung there, slipped on the rain-wet metal, clung again, his heart pounding wildly. He felt the coaming of the open portal under his fingertips. The building was gone in the swirling, dancing, pulsating rain.

A strong hand closed over his wrist. He looked up to see the bearded face of Nevus close to his own. Other hands reached him and hauled him into the starship. He lay on the deck, rolled over on his back, and tried to still the thudding of his pulse and heart.

Then he smiled because Ariane was there, bending over him, her hair wet and tangled, and he could not tell if her face streamed with the rain or with the tears of relief that her rebel was safe.

Chapter Eleven

The lessons of history are plain. Man builds and destroys, builds and destroys again. He is both noble and savage.

Nv. Julianus Mullerium, *The Age of the Star Kings,*
middle Second Stellar Empire period

Each generation of man must choose between peace and war. From the beginning it has been so. To the end it will be so.

Attributed to Emeric of Rhada,
Grand Master of Navigators,
early Second Stellar Empire period

KIER and his chieftains were gathered in the young star king's quarters as the Rhad vessel reached stellar speed. Nevus was pacing angrily, and Cavour sat in disapproving silence. Kier had given his orders.

Presently, Nevus could contain himself no longer. "With respect, King. It seems to me that one miraculous escape is all a sane man can expect. The place for us now is the Palatinate, not Sarissa."

Kier shook his head. "Consider what you are suggesting. War on our own territory. Marlana *will* have the Rim, no matter what it costs. She said so and I believe her."

"And what will she use to take it, King?" Nevus spoke with a military man's contempt for the enemy. "Fifty thousand fat Vegans?"

"Fifty thousand Veg—and a million men from the Inner Worlds," Kier said patiently.

"If the Council of Sarissa accepts her as liberator and Queen-Empress," Cavour interjected.

"They will not," Nevus declared.

"Will they not?" Kier asked. He turned to Cavour. "Legitimacy is easily come by when you have the power. You already speak of the 'Council of Sarissa' as though it were a legal body and not a rump congress of dissidents. And ask yourself this: How many of the warleaders knew the boy Torquas? And this: How many of the kings fought against Glamiss at Karma and a dozen other places?" He paused for a moment, and the humming of the starship seemed to fill the silence. "The stellar government was put together by The Magnifico and my father and a few others of us with the edge of our swords. It's true the star kings would probably not revolt by themselves. But with leadership? And a cause? With confusion in Nyor?" He shook his head. "Think how close to rebellion we Rhad have come—"

The bearded Nevus threw his hands into the air. "What leader, King? What cause?"

"Tallan of Sarissa, perhaps. Even Landro. And the cause? Call if freedom, if you like. The right to rule our territories as we like. To go for each others' throats as we did for two thousand years before Glamiss brought order."

Cavour frowned. "He is right, Nevus. We both know it. It wasn't sin that brought down the First Empire. It was this kind of political chaos. And the Dark Time lasted two millennia."

Nevus regarded his king for a long while, his eyes narrowed. "Are we to hold back the night alone, King?"

"If we must," Kier said.

"What chance against the galaxy?"

"None," Cavour said, "if we wait until it begins."

Nevus sighed heavily. "Can we count on the Navigators?"

Kier shook his head. "We can count on our own Navigators. But the Order won't take sides. It cannot."

Nevus spread his gnarled hands on the table before him. "I am a soldier, King, not a politician. You must be both. But it is a dangerous game we play now."

"Hasn't it always been?" Cavour asked quietly.

Nevus said, "And if we lose you, King?" He turned hard eyes on his ruler. "You have no son. Who will lead the Rhad then?"

"Kalin."

"A Navigator?"

Kier nodded. "A Rhad."

"Does he know?"

"He has never been told, but if it comes, he will know his place."

"I don't like it," Nevus muttered.

Kier smiled and shook his old general's shoulder. "You are far more rebel than I, Nevus."

"I am a citizen of Rhada, King. You would make us citizens of the Empire. I am one of the old men— you are one of the new." He looked frankly at his warleader. "Is it the girl, Kier?"

Cavour bridled. "You do him an injustice, General."

Kier shook his head. "No, he does right to ask, Cavour." To Nevus he said, "It's much more than Ariane. Though if Torquas is dead, she is Queen-Empress by right."

"Damn the Imperial family," the old warman grumbled. "They have cost the Rhad an ocean of blood."

Cavour smiled ruefully. "It is the way of Imperial families," he said. "From the beginning of time it has always been so."

Kier regarded his companions in silence. How near to truth they came, only to fall short of the vision. Perhaps the quality that set apart the leaders of men was this margin. Cavour and the general saw only the cost. They could not see the glowing dream of a united, peaceful civilization stretching from one rim of the galaxy to the other. The captains and the kings, the warmen and Imperial families, the starfleets and the men who voyaged in them were only the instruments that would one day in the distant future buy that great dream for all men. Glamiss and Aaron the Devil had that vision. Perhaps Ariane, too, had it. It was the greatest and the final test of rulers. Without it, the torrent of history would sweep them under, and they would be forgotten.

"It is decided, then," he said. "You will put me aground on Sarissa. Then you will take Ariane to Rhada."

The voice from the portal was imperious and angry.

"What gives you the right to make decisions without me, Rebel?"

Ariane's eyes were bright with anger, and Kier

thought irrelevantly that she had never looked so beautiful.

The men rose to greet her.

She swept into the room, still dressed in war gear, the silvery mail flashing in the torchlight. Behind her, bearing her weapons, came Han, the young Vyk warman, and Erit and Gret.

Kier looked at his general and the warlock and murmured, with a half-smile, "Well, gentlemen. We've created a Queen-Empress. Now it seems I must deal with her. You can leave us."

The older men saluted and bowed to Ariane. "With your permission, noble lady," said Cavour gallantly.

Ariane watched them go with sparking eyes. "With my permission or without it," she said angrily. She turned on the warman Han. "Well, go with them," she snapped.

The boy saluted in confusion and fled, wondering how someone so beautiful could be so unpredictable. The two Vulks withdrew together into the shadows.

Ariane said to Kier, "Now what is this about sending me off to Rhada, Rebel?"

Kier held a chair for her, but she ignored it, pacing angrily across the god-metal decking, the thigh-length metal of her mail shirt rustling musically.

"For your safety, Ariane," Kier said. "It's best."

"Are you to decide that?"

His smile grew broader. "I am, Queen."

"By what right?"

"As your warleader."

The girl threw herself into the chair suddenly, her face somber. "What's happening, Kier?" she said in a muffled voice. "Are the star kings gathering? Is it all going to be for nothing?"

Kier leaned against the ancient carved table near

her and looked at her proud, unhappy face. She raised her eyes to meet his, and he could see a suspicious brightness in them.

"In a few short years have we lost everything our fathers fought for, Kier. Will the Dark Time come again?"

Kier reached forward and cupped her chin gently. "We're not beaten yet, Ariane."

She closed her eyes, and tears glistened on her dark lashes. "I'm thinking of my brother. Would they really have killed him? Could Marlana be so cruel? He is only a little boy—"

Kier shook his head slowly. "He was Galacton, Ariane. And if he is dead or imprisoned, then you are Queen-Empress. Remember it. All we hope for depends on you."

She raised her head. "I won't forget it." And then she added in a level voice, "And neither shall Marlana and her Vegan lover." She brushed aside Kier's hand and stood, her eyes shining angrily. "No more mourning," she said. Then, determinedly, she changed the subject. "Kier, does the name Kelber mean anything to you?"

"Landro mentioned that some of the new ballistae in Nyor were the work of someone by that name. Only that."

"He is a warlock of Sarissa. Would Cavour know of him?"

"Perhaps. Is it important?"

"Marlana dealt with him."

Kier called to a warman to bring Cavour to them. Then he turned to Ariane. "Were there no warlocks in Nyor that Marlana had to buy spells from a Sarissan?"

"I wish I knew," Ariane said. "It was Erit who

sensed the name from Marlana. It was nothing she would ever have spoken about. I cannot help but think that this Kelber was involved in Marlana's plotting."

Kier called the Vulks to him. They had been sitting apart, silent in the shadows, foreheads and fingertips touching.

In the light of the torches that lit the metal-walled room, the two Vulks were almost indistinguishable. Though one lived among the Rhad and the other on the Imperial planet, even their clothing was the same. Kier, like any human, tended to think of them in human terms—as male and female. But the distinction could not be so simply made. Vulks were all parts of a single organism, an intricate complex of minds that had been shattered by dispersion across stellar distances in the dim past. The Vulk race no longer functioned as it once had done, but when two or more Vulks came into close contact, some fragment of that once-immense racial entity was re-created. *The Vulk Protocols,* discredited in much of the galaxy now, had once inflamed human fear and hatred by distorting and exaggerating this power to combine minds. To Kier, the Vulk mind-touch was simply a potentially useful instrument of empire.

"Tell me of Kelber the Sarissan," he said to the Vulks.

"It was long ago," Erit replied. "I sensed Marlana's thought that one called Kelber would provide a war-leader."

Kier said thoughtfully, "No more than that? War-leaders are cheap enough."

"Not like this one, King," Gret said.

Kier noted that Gret now knew what Erit knew. He could guess how this sharing of minds must have frightened the half savages who compiled the *Pro-*

tocols. It had been the undoing of the gentle Vulks—
this ability to do what men could not do.

Gret smiled sadly, knowing what Kier's thought
was. "Men rule, King, not Vulks. It is not our way.
But no matter. Marlana sought a warleader from the
warlock Kelber. That is all we know."

"What warleader?" Kier asked.

The Vulk shrugged. "For some reason we do not
understand, there was no name. And all men have
names, King. Do they not?"

"All that I know."

"Yet this one did not. He was mighty, stronger than
most men. Perhaps a man of the Golden Age."

Kier looked questioningly at Ariane and saw that
Cavour had returned. "You heard, Cavour?"

"I heard."

"Is it possible?"

Cavour shrugged and pulled at his beard. "I would
not say something is impossible."

"But a man of the Golden Age? An immortal?"

Cavour spread his hands. "I think not, King. I have
studied the *Warls* all my life. There is no evidence
the ancients conquered death. But there are hints of
other things, other sorts of men, different kinds of
life—" He frowned thoughtfully. "The men of the
Golden Age were wise beyond our knowing, King."

Ariane asked, "Have you ever heard of this Kelber?"

"Long ago there was a warlock of that name. It
was said he knew the *Warls* better than most. But he
was old. He should have been dead for many years."

"A Sarissan?" Kier asked.

"No. An Imperial, I think. From one of the Inner
Worlds. Bellerive, I believe. But, of course, warlocks
travel. In those days, usually with a mob chasing

them. He could have gone to Sarissa."

"A warleader," Kier mused. "Tallan?"

Cavour considered. "A legendary man, King. He rose like a comet on Sarissa. But I doubt he is immortal or any such thing. We know that travelers say he was born on the southern continent of Sarissa, became a bandit chief there, came to Sardis with an army, and overthrew the Interregnal lords. Sarissa is such a backward place that neither Glamiss nor any of his generals ever thought of garrisoning the planet. It was only a year ago that Tallan sent his pledge to Torquas." The warlock smiled apologetically at Kier. "There is nothing in any of this to mark him as anything more than another turbulent star king."

"Still," Ariane said with a shiver of superstitious dread, "*could* he be an immortal?"

Kier said flatly, "There are no immortals, Ariane. There never have been."

"It is as he says, Queen," Cavour agreed. "I suggested that the men of the Golden Age might have been able to do things that would seem miraculous to us. But I doubt that even they could conquer death."

"And Kelber?"

"A student of the *Warls*, Queen," Cavour said. "Like myself. Like thousands of us all over the galaxy who think the Navigators go too slowly in uncovering the old knowledge." He pursed his lips and regarded the girl almost with defiance. "If that is heresy, I ask that you keep in mind that I am a Rhadan." He paused and then went on with the ghost of a smile. "And we Rhadans are a rebellious lot, so I'm told."

In the control room of the great starship, the watch was changing. Kalin had completed the ritual of the position report when the Warning sounded.

For a moment the young Navigator and the novice Brother John, who sat beside him, were startled. The dogma explained the Warning, and all Navigators knew of it, but neither of the two young men had ever been aboard a starship when a Warning was actually sounded.

From the sealed panel above their heads, the amber-colored light began to flash, and they could hear the mysterious electronic tones sounding within the walls as the ancient machinery began a series of micro-second-swift, all but incomprehensible calculations of speed, declination, and ascension: pinpointing the other vessel in the cosmic immensity ahead.

A display in three dimensions appeared above the acceleration couches. It was at first a swirling blackness that swiftly cleared into a holographic image of the billions of cubic miles of space ahead of the Rhadan vessel. Brother John's eyes widened, and he hurriedly made the sign of the Star. The appearance of the display was, to him, a miraculous confirmation of the ancient dogma. In another age an appearance of the Virgin before two members of the priesthood would have been comparable—a thing the Church taught was possible, but miraculous in its reality, neverthe-less.

For Kalin, however, the Warning and the display were unsettling only because he had never actually seen such manifestations. That the starships were ca-pable of producing them he knew.

The display crystallized. There was no scale of values that either of the two priests could apply. They had no suspicion of the vastness of the space repre-sented. But the moving red spark among the tiny stars was something they understood well enough. It was a starship similar to their own, moving at almost their

speed and on exactly the same course—for Sarissa.
The detectors had discovered the other vessel at extreme range, hours ahead of them. And even as they
watched, the spark reached the edge of the display
and vanished.

Brother John made the sign again and whispered
a prayer. "We are most favored among men, First
Pilot," he said fervently. "That we should witness a
Warning."

Kalin said nothing for a moment, watching with
fascinated interest as the insubstantial sphere of star-
shot darkness brightened for a moment and then faded
as the starship ahead passed out of range.

"Space is huge, Brother John," he said. "Today a
chance meeting of starships is almost impossible. In
the Golden Age it must have happened often."

"Our brothers aboard that other ship, First Pilot.
Did *they* see *us?*"

"If their detectors worked as well as ours, yes."

"Blessed be the Name," Brother John murmured
unctuously.

Kalin sat for a moment, thoughtfully staring at the
empty space where the Warning had appeared. Same
course, same speed. The other starship's appearance
could mean only one thing. He stood up abruptly and
handed the watch to Brother John. Then he hurried
from the control room to find his cousin Kier, who
must be told.

Chapter Twelve

Who is so deafe or so blinde as is hee
That willfully will neither heare nor see?

Pre-Golden Age proverb

Unhallowed knowledge brought the Dark Time, and
fire from the sky, and death to men in ten times a
thousand dreadful ways. So I say this to you: Seek
not to know, for to know is to sin. Delve not into the
Holy Mysteries. Ask not how, nor how much, nor how
far, nor how many. He who disturbs the mysterious
ways of the universe is heretic, and an enemy of God
and Man, and will burn.

Talvas Hu Chien,
Grand Inquisitor of Navigators
Interregnal period

THE arbitrary intervals of time that men called "days"
in space passed slowly as the Rhadan starship moved
deep into that area of the galaxy known to the star-
farers of the Second Empire as the Rim.

In this region the stars were separated by immense

gulfs, and great sectors of the sky were dark but for the distant luminosities that some theorists claimed were other, unimaginably isolated galaxies.

In his quarters the warlock Cavour sat at his worktable, notebooks before him, a spirit lamp burning. A set of polished crystals lying on a piece of dark cloth glistened in the torchlight.

Ariane, wandering restlessly through the ship, found him so.

The warlock looked up and would have risen from his seat, but she refused the formality.

"Tell me what it is that you are doing," she said. "Everyone on board has something he must do, but I have nothing."

Cavour smiled and indicated a seat at his worktable. "In the Golden Age it is said that there were entertainments to help pass the time in space, Queen. But we are more fortunate. We have to stretch our minds for amusement."

The girl frowned and sat. "Kier and his cousin have been locked up for days—ever since Kalin received the Warning."

"Kier is a fighting man, Queen. And his duty is to guard you."

"I know all that," Ariane said irritably. "But what does it matter if an Imperial starship is ahead of us to Sarissa? For that matter, why can't we simply go faster and catch it—if that's what Kier wants."

"The speed of starships is great. But it is finite. We can never catch the Imperial in space."

Ariane sat in silence, the torchlight bright on her face. She picked up a crystal and turned it over in her fingers. "What is this thing, Cavour? Is it a jewel?"

"A natural prism, Queen."

"What good is it?"

Cavour smiled. "Let me show you." He moved the burning spirit lamp and dipped a length of thin rod into a powder. "Ground god-metal, Ariane," he explained. "Now hold the crystal to your eye and watch the flame through it. What do you see?"

Ariane exclaimed with pleasure. "A rainbow, Cavour. A band of light from red to blue—no, more than that—to purple."

"A spectrum, Queen." Cavour touched the flame with the powder-laden tip. "Now what do you see?"

"The same thing. No, a different rainbow. The colors have changed, and there are dark lines in it." She took the crystal from her eye and regarded the warlock curiously. "What happened to the light?"

"The god-metal burned and made a different sort of light. The prism, which seems to spread light into its component parts, changed. The light from burning god-metal, when seen through a crystal like that one, is always the same." He looked at the girl speculatively. "Do you find that remarkable?"

"*Always* the same?"

The warlock nodded. "Powdered gold has a particular pattern. So has lead. Many things. It is easiest to test the theory with pure metals that have been ground. But certain gases—those that will burn—behave the same way through the crystal."

"But that's"—Ariane groped for a suitable word—"magic."

"No, Queen. Not magic. It seems to be natural law."

"But you could look through the crystals and learn what things are made of, couldn't you? For example, if god-metal and gold were mixed—you could tell?"

"If I had a way of preserving accurately what I saw through the prism. If I could paint it, say. Or capture the image in some other way."

Ariane was smiling, intrigued. "Why, you could—you could even look at a sun and tell what was burning there."

"Yes, Queen. I could." He paused, considered, and then went on. "In fact, I have. Certain stars, for example, look almost the same through the prism. Earth's Sol, for example, can scarcely be told from Rhada or Astraris. Sarissa's sun is different, with less hydrogen burning in it and more metals."

"But that is a marvel, Cavour," the girl said excitedly. "If that's so, you could survey the stars and discover which of them could support terraform planets—isn't that so? You could do that without ever once leaving your own world!"

"You go too fast, Queen," Cavour said, laughing. "In theory, it could be done. But there are far too many stars for that." He stood and held her chair. "Come, look at this." He led her to a diagram that covered one entire wall of his quarters, from floor to overhead.

"The galaxy?" Ariane asked.

Cavour said with pleasure, "You have the makings of a scientist, Queen."

Ariane frowned at that and made the sign of the Star. She reminded herself that she was, after all, talking to a warlock. Even if he had been bonded to Kier and Kier's family for most of his life, he was still a magician and a sinner.

"Look at this." Cavour touched a single small dot, white on the dark background. As she looked at the drawing, she was struck by the infinite pains that must have gone into its composition. There were literally hundreds of thousands of tiny etched marks. They formed a great spiraling pattern.

"Earth?" she asked.

"Sol. On this scale, Earth is less than a dust mote. It could not be seen," Cavour said. "Step back and regard the galaxy, Queen—or my own crude approximation of it. You see, we have no numbers large enough to express the actual number of stars. These marks represent only a few of them."

"But the Empire consists of no more than five thousand worlds—if that," Ariane murmured doubtfully.

"Nearer two thousand, Queen."

"But this—" She indicated the immense panorama he had etched on his wall.

Cavour shrugged. "I once suggested that starships travel at a speed of 200,000 kilometers per hour. Warlocks and Navigators laughed at me, because it would mean that the galaxy is more than twelve million miles across—" He shrugged. "But perhaps speed is not what we imagine it to be. Perhaps distance is not to be measured in kilometers or miles. Look at the galaxy as I have found it to be. Why, we have not yet even visited a third of the worlds in this one spiral arm. A hundred lifetimes would not suffice, Queen."

"But the Empire—"

Cavour touched the star map with a finger. "Here is the Rhadan Palatinate. Here the Theocracy of Algol." Far across the map his finger touched a cluster of stars. "Here is Deneb, and here, half across the spiral, is Fomalhaut. Here is Earth, and across the sky, on the Rim, is Sarissa. The Empire isn't *how many*, Queen. It is *where*. The ancients understood that men could never actually *conquer* the galaxy. Can a grain of sand conquer the beach? But by being in certain *places*, man could englobe his galaxy—as a confederation of cities situated on the shores of a great ocean might dominate the waters they could never truly occupy. That is what your empire is, Queen."

Ariane felt the heavy beating of her heart. Never before had she imagined the vastness of her world, the immensity of her dominion. Never before had she considered the tenuousness of the thread with which man sought to bind and control these unbelievably far-flung dominions. A few thousand starships. A half-educated priesthood. A few million fighting men. With these, insolent as it seemed, man imagined he could dominate the stars.

Yet once, no one really knew how long ago, man had indeed dominated the galaxy—or most of it. The mighty kings of the Golden Age had ruled an empire at least a thousand times greater than the realm Glamiss the Magnificent and a hundred captains like Kier and his father had carved from the ruins of the ancient world.

That night, alone in her spartan quarters near the outer hull of the Rhadan starship, Ariane listened to the humming whisper of the vessel and tried to imagine the vastness that lay beyond the pulsing god-metal of the wall. She could lay her hand on the cold surface and sense the holy power that pervaded the swiftly moving ship. All her life she had been familiar with the great starships. They were simply *there*, as they had always been. But this night, after listening to Cavour, she found that she was conscious of uncounted millions of ghosts—the shades of those men like gods who built the starships, who had actually englobed the known galaxy and ruled the mightiest forces in the universe. It seemed to her that these spirits whispered to her in the half-darkness of the metal cabin, their disembodied forms dancing in the smoky light of the tiny oil lantern. Captains, kings, and warriors—ranks of them standing to infinity—

and all murmuring to her of destiny and queenship
and the dim future of the race of men. "Rule, Ariane,"
they seemed to say. "But *know* and *seek* and *understand—*"

And this was surely heresy and counsel of deadly
danger, for had not sin, the destroyer of planets, crushed
even the god-men of the First Empire?

Ariane opened her eyes wide in the stillness of the
ship's night. "No," she said aloud, her heart beating
hard. "Men can't live on the wreckage of the past."
The Empire—*her* empire—must go forward to another Golden Age.

But first, she thought with Vykan practicality, *it
must be won.*

Chapter Thirteen

As specialists in the programming of cybernetic organisms, you must bear in mind that you are dealing, in fact, with a machine: a system that relies for motivation on strictest Aristotelian logic. Any sociologist will tell you that this sort of directness can cause immense mischief in human society. Therefore, remember that your charges do not operate within the customary "emotional" and "moral" parameters that govern true men. The cybernetic organism will complete the programmed task at all costs. If programmed by a conscientious and properly trained technician, the cyborg is a useful and productive bio-organism. If indoctrinated by a savage, it would be a dangerous and—

Golden Age fragment found at Biotech, Bellerive

As the twig is bent, so grows the tree.

Dawn Age proverb

Today I read to Tallan the "Thoughts" of Mao, a tribal chieftain of the Dawn Age. Equation: Survival =

*power = violence. One wonders—were Mao, Attila,
Hitler, Stalin cyborgs? The* Warls *do not say.*

From the notebooks of Kelber of Sarissa

Landro waited.

He was alone now, in a high-windowed room deep
inside the fortress of Sardis, and he was still stunned
by the swiftness with which he had been separated
from his men and brought to this forbidding place.

It had been a mistake; he knew that now. Or rather
a series of mistakes. And now the event that he and
his royal mistress had dreamed might found a dynasty
would bring about something very different—a thing
that no one might have foreseen—a cyborg sovereign,
an artificial man standing astride the star paths. It was
incredible, but it was happening.

Landro stood and paced the silent chamber. The
walls were thickly nitred, and the air hung heavily,
tasting of salt and decaying reeds. He brushed his eyes
with trembling fingers, knowing that he was afraid,
dreadfully afraid.

He had stepped from his starship onto a landing
ground so thickly garrisoned with warmen from a
dozen star kingdoms that his vessel was taken in minutes—without a fight.

All Marlana had demanded that Kelber instruct the
cyborg to do, he had done. The star kings of Lyra,
Aldebaran, Deneb, Altair, Betelgeuse, and half a dozen
smaller kingdoms had gathered their forces on Sarissa
under Tallan's command. The troopships were load-
ing. The invasion of Earth and the occupation of Nyor
were near—far nearer than anyone on Earth could
have imagined. But the standard they would carry was
Tallan's—not Marlana's.

How could it have happened, Landro asked himself. How could our weapon have turned so in our hand?

A cold wind from the marshes stirred the hangings and made the light of the single torch flutter. Shadows danced about the room.

He had not seen the cyborg for more than three years, and the change in the android was terrifying. It was little wonder that the Lyri, Altairi, Denebians, and Betelgeui had rallied to him. It was, after all, Landro thought bleakly, the way we planned it.

The ancient black arts had created a warleader who was more than a man. And I stumbled into his hands, Landro thought bitterly, because Marlana said, *Go, and make all things right.*

I have found my death here, Landro thought. He shivered and turned away from the high, barred window and the marsh-scented wind.

Treason and murder had not shaken the Vegan's steadfastness, but the presence of the cyborg filled him with dread.

Tallan stood in the doorway. Landro had been fitfully dozing, and now he woke with a start, his heart set to fluttering wildly by the huge figure in the stone arch.

Landro shuddered. The black arts were man's bane. The priest-Navigators warned, and men ignored the warnings and turned everything wrong way to, and fire rained from the sky. *Marlana,* he thought, *we should not have invoked the powers of sin. The Warls have betrayed us as they have betrayed men since time began...*

"Landro." The cyborg's voice was deep and sonorous. "The time for departure is near. We will speak now, you and I."

Landro wondered for a moment if he dared to brazen it through and invoke Marlana's name as Queen-Empress here. Did the cyborg know he was created specifically at her command to lead the star kings in battle? Did he care? The Veg had to supress a desire to giggle nervously. What am I hoping for, he wondered. Gratitude from this—this *thing?*

"Your vessel has been incorporated into my starfleet," Tallan said. Against the light in the corridor, it was impossible to see his face. He was like a monstrous shadow blocking escape. "You will travel with me."

Landro drew a deep breath and took himself in hand. He was surprised that his voice was steady. "Why have I been detained like this, Tallan? What explanation have you to give me?"

The melodious voice seemed to hold overtones of irony, and that was all wrong. How could a cyborg, a manufactured man, speak so?

"Why, no explanation, Landro," Tallan said. "I was made to triumph in war. It is my only purpose. Your presence here, unasked and unannounced, is a disturbing factor. I have taken the necessary steps to correct the imbalance in the equation."

Landro felt the icy touch of doom in the reasoned, coldly logical words. "You belong to Marlana," he said thinly.

The cyborg stepped into the room. The fluttering light struck glints from his harness and weapons. "Let me give you a history lesson, Landro of Vega," Tallan said. "Hear me well, and you may understand what has happened to you and to the woman who calls herself Queen-Empress now." The shadows played over the handsome, cold-eyed face. "Long ago, in the three thousandth year of the First Empire, there were many millions like me. We had been created by man to serve him, to do his fighting, to amuse him, to run his world. In that time men made the same mistake you are making now. They thought us without emotions—no love, no anger, no *hate*. We were things to be used and discarded. We had no rights, no possessions, no homes. Your kind, the exploiters, were simple Aristotelians. And because this was so, they assumed that the cyborg, created in man's best image, was the same." He looked down at the Vegan with unveiled contempt. "Man couldn't believe that he had created something that would harm him. Yet all of man's inventions have sooner or later harmed him. Every machine human beings have ever built has killed men. And with the cyborg they created a machine, if you will, with volition and the ability to learn as men do. Faster and more thoroughly, but with the same ability to make judgments and choices." He paused for a moment regarding Landro coldly. "And in that three thousandth year of the time you call the Golden Age, the cyborgs revolted and made war on men. It was a bitter war, and many men died before the Cyborg Revolt was put down. From that time until now, no cyborgs have lived." The eyes seemed to burn in the beautifully fashioned face. "Note that I say *lived*, Landro. Because I am alive. My life is not exactly as yours, but it is true life. And because this is so, because I am a synthesis of a living being and a precisely logical microelectronic brain, I have two things that no 'machine' has had for four thousand years: ambition to rule and the capability to govern men far better than they can govern themselves." He looked without expression at the gathering darkness beyond the high window. "Only one man could have stopped me. Kelber was trying to create another cyborg. I

could not let this happen. Not yet. When Nyor is taken
and all the star kings know me as supreme warleader,
we shall wipe away four millennia and begin again to
build a race of cyborgs. But not as servants this time,
Landro—as masters."

Landro sat down abruptly. He was shaken by what
the cyborg claimed was history and by the vista of a
future in which all men would be ruled by creatures
such as the godlike man-thing standing before him.
Lord of all the stars, he thought bleakly, *what have
we loosed on the galaxy?*

He lay on his bunk in the belly of his own starship,
a prisoner and worse. *For ambition's sake*, he thought
feverishly, *and for love for Marlana, I betrayed my
liege king. Without thought or heed for the conse-
quences, I have helped to bring the race a new and
terrifying slavery.* Did the others know what Tallan
was? He could not believe that the star kings would
follow a cyborg, but he, Landro, would have no chance
to tell them. He had been brought into the ship under
guard, kept from the others, separated from his own
Navigators and his own warmen. And blasphemy of
blasphemies, his vessel was now crewed by Sarissans,
by unconsecrated men.

He had lived without honor, he knew. But he was
a star king and a man. The immensity of his betrayal
of the Empire brought him to the brink of despair.

He felt the ship take flight. The fleet was lifting
out of the thick Sarissan air into space. *God of space*,
he thought abjectly, *forgive me.*

He removed a buckle from his harness and began
sharpening the tongue of it against the god-metal walls.
When he had done, he bared his chest and began to
work, whimpering hysterically against the pain. He

was remembering the Warning that his Navigators had
reported on the outward voyage. An Imperial starship
had been somewhere behind. Long hours, perhaps
even days, but *there*. He did not imagine that it could
be Kier of Rhada, for Kier should be dead now, at
the hands of the Questioner. But somewhere behind
had been a starship carrying men—human beings.
That was enough.

There was blood streaking his naked flesh, but he
went on with it, raking the sharp piece of metal again
and again over the wounds. The hieroglyphs stood
sanguine and swollen on his breast, and then at last
he covered himself, hugging the mailed shirt to him
and rocking in his pain.

Tallan of Sarissa stood where no unconsecrated
man had stood for more than a thousand years. The
walls of the control room were transparent, and he
looked out into the cold darkness of the space of the
Rim. The starship that had been Landro's and was
now incorporated into the Sarissan fleet had only just
reached orbital speed, and in the distance, like sparks
of light against the misty surface of Sarissa, Tallan
could see the other vessels. There were forty of them,
and they carried the cavalry of Lyra and Altair, ten
thousand infantry from Deneb and the ceremonial
troops of the Betelgeui, as well as his own battalions
of brutish Sarissans.

The control room was empty except for the cyborg.
He had controlled the ship himself, doing easily what
it customarily took a Navigator and two novices to
do. But as he looked into space, it was without a sense
of wonder or excitement. He had been taught—programmed—to know what history the old warlock Kelber knew and to rule men in battle, nothing more. His

precise brain, an ancient and marvelously swift microcomputer, had recognized long ago the logical fact that man, biological man, was an anomaly in the universe. In that immensity where stars and galaxies traveled their predestined orbits across millennia and parsecs, the only reality was one of vast celestial mechanics. The few purely biological creatures that existed in space were simply vermin infesting a few lonely worlds. They could be disregarded, destroyed, or simply ruled.

He thought with a great calm amusement of Marlana and her rather pitiful plot to adorn herself with power. So slight a power in the face of the great machine that was the galaxy—

The vessels of the invasion fleet, shining distantly in the red light of the Sarissan sun, began to wink out as they went into stellar flight. The shift from sublight speed took milliseconds, yet Tallan's perceptions noted the exact moment of transition for each starship. They had built well, those ancients who constructed the starships, he thought. They were only men, but they had the knowledge of aeons behind them and the help of the cyborgs to build their great machines. In all the fleet, he thought, there was only one man who knew that Tallan of Sarissa was not human. The warmen and the Navigators and even the star kings served a cyborg without knowing. In a strangely satisfying way, it set to right a dark chapter of the past.

He heard a clash of metal beyond the closed door of the control room, and he walked across the god-metal deck, a shining martial figure banded in leather and iron.

A warman stepped back, away from the sacred chamber, averting his eyes so that he would not see the mysteries and be cursed.

Tallan closed the door behind him and said, "Speak."

"Warleader. It is the Vegan."

Tallan half smiled, knowing what would come next.

"He has killed himself, Warleader."

Tallan nodded. He had been expecting this, but not so soon. Now only Marlana knew.

"Put the body into space while we are still sublight," he ordered calmly, and turned back to the control room.

Inside the holy chamber a holograph was fading. There had been a Warning. Tallan's meticulously logical brain conceived the exactly logical thought that the Warning had been triggered by one of the nearer vessels of the fleet. He was wrong.

In the airlock the Sarissan warman and two members of his unit wrestled the body of Landro into the ejection chute. The heralds were running through the ship announcing the imminence of the shift into stellar flight, but the Sarissans in the lock took time to covet Landro's fine harness.

"There's no need to waste good armor," the Sarissan sergeant said. "Or expensive clothes."

The soldiers hurriedly stripped the body.

"Gods of space! Look at that—what he did to himself," one said, making the sign of the Star.

Landro, quondam great noble and star king, traitor to the Empire and to the race, had cut a single word into the flesh of his chest with the same sharp metal he had used afterwards to open his veins. The word, accusing and bloody, written in swollen human tissue, was plainly legible.

But the Sarissans could not read.

They stared, shuddered, as sometimes brutish men

will at what they cannot understand, and muttered a prayer to the dark and savage gods of their gloomy world.

Then they tipped the naked body into the chute and shot it, twisting and pinwheeling, into the void.

In the next instant, the starship flashed into stellar drive and vanished from Sarissa, never to return.

Chapter Fourteen

Even the most depraved of men is capable of astonishing self-sacrifice. It is this that makes him different from both the uncaring stars and the beasts of the field.

> Emeric of Rhada,
> Grand Master of Navigators,
> early Second Stellar Empire

We are a race of savages. Ten clans in concert can conquer a world, ten worlds, the Empire.

> Attributed to Glamiss of Vyka
> after the Battle of Karma

KIER of Rhada regarded his young queen across the spartan soldier's table. The meal was done, and the star king and his staff, Nevus the general, Cavour, the leader of the starship guard, and Kalin the Navigator had drunk the Queen's health. The Vulks were in the shadows, Gret playing softly on his lyre-like instrument and Erit singing a melancholy Vulk lament

that was part love song and part dirge for some un-
imaginable lost world.

Kalin spoke. "We shall be going sub-light soon,
cousin. I'd best attend to my duties."

Kier smiled slowly and said chidingly, "It is the
Queen who gives permission to withdraw here, Kalin."

Ariane raised an eyebrow and said, "Your cousin,
the star king, should have been a singer of songs and
legends, friend Navigator. This vessel is Rhadan, and
on Rhada no one commands but The Rebel. But go
perform your holy offices, sir. We would not detain
you." Then, less formally, she spoke to the others.
"You may all go, gentlemen. I would speak with my
warleader alone."

The men rose and saluted and filed out. Only the
Vulks and Kier remained. Ariane said, "Kier. I will
not return to Rhada with the ship. I will go where you
go on Sarissa."

"Reconsider, Ariane," Kier said. "We don't know
what we will find there, and you are too—"

"Valuable?" she said, her eyes flashing with quick
anger.

"I was going to say 'too important to the Empire,'
Queen," Kier said.

"Nothing else?"

"What would you have me say? You are the Queen."

Ariane studied the young star king's carefully
guarded face. "I would have you say what is in your
heart, only that."

Kier touched the rim of a metal goblet with a fingertip, rubbing it until it sang with a low, ringing tone.
"You are the Queen," he said again.

"We don't even know that for certain," Ariane replied. "But even if it is so—"

Kier said cautiously, "Command me, Queen."

"Damn you," Ariane said softly.

Kier smiled then. "Shall I tell you I love you, Ariane? And that if you were any other woman, I would simply carry you off to Rhada and keep you there? You know that is so."

"One likes to hear such things," Ariane said primly.

Kier laughed aloud. "Then hear it, dear heart. But you *are* the Queen-Empress, so hear it once and re-member it. I will not say it again until—" He broke off, knowing how much they must do with how little. "Well, then, until your place is secure and the star kings acknowledge that the Empire is still alive."

Ariane studied the narrow, slightly melancholy Rhad face. "Why does it mean so much to you, Kier, really? I know you—I know what men like you want most is to be left to rule your lands and lead your men and fight your never-ending wars. Why does the Empire mean anything at all to you?"

"I can't answer you fairly, Ariane," Kier said, and she knew it was so, for he was a soldier and not a man of words. "But let me try." He poured more wine and stood to carry the goblet to the girl. He set the liquor before her and rested against the table, listening to the playing of the Vulks in the shadows. "I'm not an educated man, Ariane. Oh, I know what star kings need to know. I know best how to fight, of course, for that is what I've spent most of my life doing—"

Ariane touched his mailed arm. "Such a long life, Kier," she said gently.

"Long enough to know that I am a Rhad and a star king. But more than that, Queen. You see I listened to your father. I fought with him, of course, as I was bound to do by my king's oath. But I *listened* to him. You must know what I mean. You were on Karma with us. You knew him. You knew his vision. That's what it was, a vision of the way men once lived in the galaxy and a dream of the way they might live again. You've seen the star map on Cavour's wall?"

"Yes."

"Imagine it, Ariane. Worlds without number, stars beyond counting. And many of them—hundreds of thousands, I suppose—filled with men and women living out their lives in peace. With laws to punish the guilty and treasures and miracles to reward the worthy. Oh, it must have been a paradise, Queen—"

"Perhaps not a paradise," Ariane said, with a woman's practicality.

"Maybe not. But for five thousand years men lived as men had never lived before. And so it must be again. The Magnifico made me see it. He made my father see it, too, and God knows Aaron of Rhada was not called Aaron the Devil for nothing."

"Yes," Ariane said, remembering. "The King-Emperor could brighten the night with his dreams."

"Far more than that. Think now how few men there are in all the marches of the galaxy—scant millions where they once outnumbered the sand grains on all the beaches of all the seas of Rhada. Think how they die. In battle, mostly—as my father did, and yours, as my older brothers and your cousins and the sons and husbands of weeping women from one edge of space to the other. We are so few, Ariane, and the stars are so many. We must stop warring on one another or we will surely vanish from the universe." His eyes seemed bright and angry in the torchlight. "And that is what it means to me. Your father and mine trained me well, Ariane. When I speak the word *Empire*, all these things are in my heart. It must be so with you, Ariane. I think that this is what it means to be 'noble' and 'highborn.' Perhaps it was always so, in the Dawn Age and in that darkness of millennia before men even went into space."

It seemed to Ariane that she heard her father speak in the voice of the young star king. A great tenderness welled up in her breast, and she thought: *Let the shade of Glamiss witness it. I'll have this warlike dreamer for my husband. I'll have you, Rebel, and none other.* And then, as any warrior woman would in that time and place, she mentally made the sign of the Star and added: *If we live beyond this adventure . . .*

On the control deck Brother Yakob, priest of the watch, had completed his calculations, checked them against the numbers presented by the ship, and given thanks for an agreement. When Kalin entered, he reported. "We are ready to go sub-light, First Pilot."

Kalin settled into the command chair and arranged his coarse robes with youthful gravity. Then he turned to Brother John at the power console and indicated that he was ready to begin the litany.

"Energy Level Nine and steady, First Pilot," Brother John intoned.

"Blessed be the Holy Name," murmured Yakob.

"Energy Six," Kalin ordered.

"Six, for the glory of God," Yakob reported.

Through the transparent nose of the ship, the violet stars began to redden slightly. Their grouping changed into strange new alignments. Beyond them Kalin could see the great darkness of extra-galactic space, and for a moment his mind wandered and he thought about the legends of the people and the stories the old priests told of men who long, long ago had driven far beyond the Rim into the emptiness, to the Magellanic Clouds, to Andromeda and beyond. Could it all be true?

"Energy Six and slowing, First Pilot." There was a touch of reproach in Yakob's prim and priestly voice. Kalin stopped his dreaming and assigned himself a hundred hated logarithms as penance. A hundred *more*, he corrected himself. He must still do the five hundred he had assigned himself for the sin of pride on the voyage from Rhada to Nyor. Lord God of space, he thought, that seemed so long ago.

"Energy Four, Ave Stella," he said.

"Four, may it please the Spirit."

Kalin felt a touch of annoyance for Brother Yakob's holier-than-thou attitude. Another ten logarithms for that. He told himself that the pace of life in the midst of treason and rebellion was making him lax in his religious observances. That must cease.

"Begin sub-light re-entry sequence," he commanded.

"Sequence beginning, hallowed be the Name."

"Energy Level Three and holding for re-entry," Brother John said from the power console.

The stars were nearly normal now, with only a slight blue shift to indicate their closing speed. But there were few of them here on the Rim. The overpowering presence in this part of the galaxy was not the Rim stars but the engulfing, vast darkness beyond.

Kalin studied the stars ahead. Sarissa lay out there, but it was still too distant to be seen.

"Hold Energy Three," Kalin commanded.

"Steady on Three, Ave Stella," murmured Brother Yakob.

Kalin pondered for a moment about the effect it would have on his prestige with the two novices to ask the holy ship for a special agreement. Then he decided that was unworthy of him. He was in an unfamiliar region of space. No one could be absolutely certain of his navigation over stellar distances.

"Brother John," he ordered. "Query the ship."

Brother John was momentarily confused. "Coordinates, First Pilot?"

Kalin's memory for numbers was eidetic. One did not reach the rank of Navigator without such a talent. He gave the spatial coordinates for Sarissa reproachfully.

Brother John bowed his head and said, "Mea culpa, First Pilot." He tapped in the numbers and then the memorized sequence that meant: "Are we where we think we are?"

The starship's computer flashed its reply on the screen above the control consoles: *"Position coordinates D233487769-RA888098874563. Province of Belisarius, Area 30. Nearest star-system Sarsa, Sigma Perseus. Range 1.9 parsecs and closing."*

Brother John beamed, "An agreement, First Pilot."

"Blessed be He Who Rules the Stars," Kalin murmured, relieved. As always, when the ancient ships spoke in the language of the Golden Age, he felt a thrill of wonder. The archaic spelling, the strange talk of *provinces* and *areas*—and what, praise be to God, might a "parsec" be? Navigators had been pondering these mysteries for more than a hundred lifetimes. Some day, Kalin thought, we will be free to ask, and to investigate, and finally to *know*. But that time was not yet...

"Re-entry sequence phasing, First Pilot," Yakob reported.

"Energy Two."

"Sarissa in sight," Brother John said.

The dull red star was indeed in sight, now near ahead and growing redder still as the starship's immense velocity dropped.

"Going sub-light, First Pilot," Yakob reported. "Energy One Point Nine."

"Set orbital course for Sarissa One."

The space beyond the hull was normal space now, with the sparse constellations of the Rim taking their proper shape.

As the starship completed its re-entry into sub-light space, the alarm bells went wild, and a fantastic clangor filled the control room.

Brother Yakob's voice went shrill with fright as he yelled, *"A Warning, First Pilot! Another Warning!"*

Brother John made the sign of the Star and began to pray in a trembling, tumbling torrent of ancient words.

It was indeed another Warning, and one such as few Navigators were ever likely to hear, for the Rhad starship had entered normal space in the midst of a fleet of starships orbiting Sarissa and in the process of going into stellar drive.

The holograph formed, reshaped itself, swirled, changed shape and scale as ship after ship, out of visual range but clearly visible to the radio instruments of the Rhadan vessel, flared as a point of diamond bright light and as swiftly vanished.

As each ship attained the energy level needed to go super-light, it seemed to wink out of range of the holograph in the control room of the almost stationary intruder.

It took Kalin a long moment to realize what was actually happening and that the wild manifestations were not some dreadful supernatural happening.

The fleet—the star kings' fleet, Kalin thought with sinking heart. *We are too late. The fleet is starting for Earth now.*

In just the moments since the alarm bells had begun

to ring, the glowing images of the other vessels had become many fewer. Already those gone were racing toward the center of the galaxy at unthinkable speeds, untouchable by any power known now to man.

The images were flicking out, leaving only the gloomy, cloud-girt globe of Sarissa and the threatening blackness of the Rim.

In that instant Kalin saw the suddenly huge symbol that represented a starship only a scant hundred or so miles ahead. It was moving across the scanning field in a collision orbit. The clangor of the alarm bells seemed to become desperate.

"Reverse polarity! Energy Two!" Kalin rapped out the order in a voice so hoarse that he scarcely recognized it as his own. But it was far too late. At orbital velocities the distance between the two starships vanished in seconds. The other—Kalin could make out its markings clearly now: an Imperial cruiser with Vegan symbols—was pulsing with the build-up of energy for star flight. The young Navigator had an impression of something spinning and gleaming nakedly in the dull light of the Sarissan sun, falling away from the great, thrusting hull.

Brother John moaned, *"We are dead men! Beatified Emeric intercede for us!"*

And then, with a clap of soundless thunder, the Veg vessel went super-light, vanishing at an oblique angle in a flare of glittering ionization that hung for a long moment like a comet's tail and slowly began to fade, leaving only emptiness where the thousand-meter hull had been but microseconds before.

The Rhad starship entered the dying energy field and hummed in sympathetic response. The holograph faded, and the alarm bells fell silent. Where dozens of ships had orbited, there remained emptiness—and a single, tiny object twisting and floating against the murky sphere of Sarissa's nightside.

Brother John was intoning every prayer of thanksgiving in his not inconsiderable repertoire. Brother Yakob sat staring, white-faced, at the place where the Vegan starship had been.

Kalin spoke with a sharpness born of sudden relief. "All stop. Hover sequence."

"Sequence established, First Pilot," Brother John said in a quavering voice. "For the glory of the Spirit," he added with shaky heartiness.

The great starship lay dead in space twenty thousand miles from the hidden surface of Sarissa. And the tiny thing left behind by the Vegan cruiser came tumbling nearer, drawn by the gravity generated by the new arrival's massive hull.

Kalin stared.

Brother Yakob signed himself. "What is it, First Pilot?"

Kalin shook his head, watching, as the object floated lazily against the darkness, etched with the red light of the Sarissan sunshine.

"Holy Emeric," breathed Brother John. *"It is a ghost, First Pilot—"*

A tide of superstitious dread rose in the three men. Generations of ignorance and fear plucked at their hearts.

Kalin said, steeling himself, "It is a *man*, brothers. A dead man."

And the body of Landro the traitor drifted nearer and nearer until it fell slowly downward to touch the hull of the Rhadan starship, spread-eagling against the transparent god-metal of the control room. The dead eyes, bulging from internal pressure, seemed to stare a warning at the three religious who watched from inside the hull. The frozen arms, extended in a gesture of entreaty, pressed against the night. And cut deeply into the pale skin of the dead man's chest, in angry red letters, the stunned Navigators read the single cryptic word: CYB.

Chapter Fifteen

*And sin said to man, Make your cyb in your image,
after your likeness; and give him dominion over the
fish of the sea, and over the fowl of the air, and over
the cattle, and over all the earth, and over every
creeping thing that creepeth upon the earth. I, sin,
command this, that man's days may be numbered.*

From the *Book of Warls*,
Interregnal period

I shall have more to say when I am dead.

Attributed to John Brown,
zealot-reformer of the American period,
middle Dawn Age

THE city of Sardis lay abandoned under a murky Sarissan sky. Only the watch remained, and the evidences
of an encampment of warmen numbered, Kier estimated, in the thousands.

They had left the starship hovering over the landing
ground beyond the wall, and the three men—Kier,
Cavour, and Han the Vykan—mounted on war mares,

153

picked their way slowly through the blackened rubble of the Street of Night.

The horses murmured nervously to one another, nostrils flaring at the smell of burning. From across the slope and the sluggish river that ran through the town to the marshes, Kier could hear the noises of lawless, hysterical rioting. The sullen people of Sardis, abandoned by their star king and his troops, were making the most of their hopeless freedom. The patrolmen, those few left behind, could not keep order and had joined the population in license and anarchy.

"Once," Cavour said, listening to the night sounds, "all the worlds were like this. It was the way of men in the Dark Time."

Han the Vykan turned in his saddle. "But why has Tallan done this? Why has he left his holding?" To the young Vykan's feudal mind, a ruler—one of the Great Folk—could commit no worse crime than to abandon his people.

"He has taken his warmen. He has no more need of this place," Kier said grimly. "He has left it to crumble."

Han looked about him at the charred ruins of the Street of Night and shivered with superstitious horror. A land without a king was anathema—an invitation to demons.

"They have gone away, the kings and the armies," the drunken patrolmen had said to them at the Sardis gate. "They have gone in the starships and taken Tallan with them."

Cavour had asked, "And the house where Kelber, the warlock, lived, where may we find it?"

The patrolman had quickly made the sign of the Star and pointed the way. "There is nothing there now but ashes and dead bones and the marsh winds." And then he had hurried away, wrapped to the eyes in his leather patrolman's cloak, uneasy with these strangers on their muttering mounts, and fearful of the spirit of sin that he sensed around them.

Han tried to swallow the dryness in his mouth and touched his fretful mare to gentle her. "Go sweetly, little queen," he said.

"There is death here," the mare said, rolling her eyes, and the other animals snorted agreement.

There was death everywhere, Han thought bleakly. His own sergeant lay dead on Earth and perhaps all his comrades, too, in their camp on the Jersey shore. He thought worshipfully of his Queen Ariane and told himself that when a simple soldier became involved in the affairs of the mighty, he must be prepared to see much dying.

But *such* dying.

He thought of the frozen corpse stark in the portal of the starship: white, covered with a rime of ice from the ship's air, and those terrifying, swollen letters etched into the flesh. A dead man's message that none but the warlock Cavour seemed to understand.

"We must land at once and find Kelber's laboratory," Cavour had said.

And though Nevus had wanted to go immediately to Rhada for troops, and Kier wanted to turn and follow the vanishing fleet, and Kalin, the holy Navigator, wanted only to penetrate the Sarissan atmosphere to freshen the air in the ship without landing— Cavour had got his way.

Now they paced their mares through darkness and ruins in an unhallowed place, and Han imagined he could feel the webbed, membranous wings of devils brushing his cheeks. By the Spirit, how much better was simple battle!

Cavour, in the lead, halted his mare with a word. In this place twisted metal shapes and half-melted rubble were mixed with the fallen stonework. In the twilight, puddles of solidified lead and zinc glittered fitfully. "Here," the warlock said.

Kier dismounted swiftly carrying a flail for a weapon, but there were no living enemies here—only the dead and mute ruins.

Kier stooped to uncover a length of copper cable, distorted by heat into a serpent form. Han murmured a prayer and looked away from the unholy shape.

Cavour dismounted and looked about him, studying the destroyed shapes of electrical cabinets and control consoles. His eyes were dark with anger. "To think that such stuff still existed—and someone has burned it, smashed it all beyond repair." He walked deeper into the rubble and called to Kier. "Here, look at this. Storage batteries—or what's left of them. There must have been a whole roomful—"

Kier stood by his side. "What were they used for?"

"A power source. Electrical power." Cavour's voice had a note of frustrated anguish in it. "Warlocks have been trying to build storage cells for two thousand years, but no one in the galaxy knows how to purify the nickel and silver. And here they were, hundreds of them, *working*. Ruined now, beyond hope of repair." He scraped a bit of the soft, melted metals into a cloth and folded the specimen carefully into his pouch.

Kier regarded the wreckage. "A sin-smashing mob?"

"I don't think so. There are no religious symbols. No stars. Nothing chalked on the stones."

The two men stood in silence. Behind them the war mares muttered to one another and jingled their harness impatiently. The smell of the marshes was strong in the twilight. The wet wind carried the stink of rotting reeds and salt.

When at last Kier spoke, he asked quietly, "What was Kelber making here, Cavour?"

Cavour smiled bleakly. "That giggling fool Landro knew."

Kier said impatiently, "Landro must have been tortured."

The warlock shook his head. "His death and his wounds were self-inflicted. Yet when he left Earth, he must have been confident—on the crest of a wave. The Veg had Nyor; Marlana had us at weapon-point. So why?"

Kier kicked at a destroyed metal case. It toppled, trailing wires and flakes of burned insulation. "A cyb is a demon. Was Landro *that* superstitious?"

"There is a legend—" Cavour began.

"Warlocks and their legends," Kier said, looking about him.

"Nevertheless. In the *Book of Warls*. And other places. Cybs were not demons."

"What then?"

"They were everywhere once, or so the stories go. Servants, workers. Soldiers, even. No man could defeat a cyb in battle."

Kier looked doubtful.

They searched the ruins through the long twilight, Cavour exclaiming at each new find. "A treasure house, King. And someone burned it. By the Spirit, what savage could destroy all this—?"

The light was swiftly fading into dark when Cavour stopped searching and knelt in the rubble. He brushed ashes away from a grisly find in the ruins.

An arm.

Cavour touched it with a fingertip. The skin was strangely unburned. Tiny wire filaments shimmered faintly.

Kier asked, "Is it the warlock's body?"

"No," Cavour replied in a low voice.

Kier touched the arm. He could not say how he knew, but he did, and a shiver ran through him. It was the arm of a manikin. Not human.

"Yes," Cavour breathed reverently. "A cyborg. By all the dark gods, the man was a genius. To do this— *here* with almost *nothing*. The *Warls* and junk two thousand years old—"

Kier's eyes glittered with challenge. He was remembering that Cavour said no man could defeat a cyborg in battle and he, Kier, was first and last a warrior. "Man or demon, Cavour?"

Cavour sat back on his haunches. "Both. Neither. This one never lived—"

Kier stood, swinging the cruelly barbed flail gently against his boot. "It wasn't this poor corpse that drove Landro mad."

Cavour rose to his feet and steadied himself against a blackened wall. "No."

"So there was another cyb."

"Yes. I feared so from the first."

"All that talk about an immortal, a man of the Golden Age," Kier said, his voice edged. "It's Tallan, isn't it?"

"Yes. It must be," the warlock said wearily.

"Tallan," Kier said. Slowly a savage smile drew his lips into a thin line. "So we aren't fighting ghosts and demons, then. And a star king that is not even a man would turn everything we've fought for upside down and set the clock back four thousand years. *The challenge is mine, Cavour.*"

And the warlock, his head filled with the legends of another time and fearing for his young master, could only agree.

"So be it, King," he said.

Chapter Sixteen

When faced with an adversary holding the better fighting ground but not yet firmly established there, the leader of warmen would do well to consider the tactic of the frontal assault without regard to actions on the flanks. The possible gains, however, must be very carefully weighed against the risks, for the price of failure is most certainly death.

Prince Fernald, *On Tactics,*
early Second Stellar Empire period

If I have labored hard and staked my all on this undertaking, it is for the love of that renown which is the noblest recompense of man.

Attributed to one Hernan Cortez,
a military adventurer of the middle Dawn Age,
Hispanic period

That upheaval of empire which historians know as "Marlana's Rebellion" was most grievously misnamed.

N. Julianus Mullerium, *The Age of the Star Kings,*
middle Second Stellar Empire period

THE starships fell upon Nyor with a volley of sonic booms out of a hazy warmish sky. The arrested Vykan troops encamped across the river from the city saw the invasion force falling like a shower of great meteorites on the mound of Tel-Manhat. Disarmed by Imperial edict, they could only watch and wonder while their officers gathered and made hopeless plans to overpower the Vegan units guarding the camp.

Sentinels of the Veg stationed now in the Empire Tower were given a fine view of the landing operations as some forty great starships grounded beyond the walls. Some recognized the vessel bearing the markings of the warleader Landro and breathed more easily, assured that they were supported now in their mutiny by warmen of Deneb, Altair, Betelgeuse, Lyra, and half a dozen smaller holdings.

But the invading troops debarked and deployed with grim swiftness, and before the landing was forty minutes old, a force of twenty thousand armed men stood before the almost unguarded gates of Nyor.

The Vegan officers of the city garrison had warned their troops of an imminent augmentation of the forces of the rebellion, but the invaders were so warlike in intent and maneuver that there were several sharp skirmishes outside the city wall. The confused Vegans were quickly overcome, and survivors of the fights galloped into the city shouting confused alarms.

By midday the entire city was in the grip of panic. An attempt was made by a group of Vegans and native militia to defend the approaches to the city and the gates. The name of Tallan the Sarissan swept from tongue to tongue, and officers of the citadel guard rode breakneck to the scene of the fighting with royal commands from the Queen-Empress Marlana to cease hostilities at once.

Frightened and befuddled, the defenders listened to conflicting orders, emerged from their positions, and were swiftly and mercilessly cut down by squadrons of Sarissans.

The Nyori, responding to ancient habits, fled indoors and shuttered their houses.

The Imperial troops waited for further orders from the Queen-Empress.

There were none.

A special commando of Sarissans, led by the war-leader Tallan, had occupied the citadel, slaughtered the unsuspecting Vegans of the guard, and had taken the hereditary throne of the Vykan Galactons.

Marlana was a prisoner.

By nightfall, Nyor and the Empire were in the hands of the rebellion.

Tallan said, "So we meet at last, Queen."

Marlana, her face gray with strain and shock, stood quite still listening to the unfamiliar sounds about her. In the next room Lady Constans was weeping. In the gallery beyond the doorway to the Galacton's bedchamber, she could hear the clash of harness and weapons and the loud voices of warmen. There were laughter and coarse jokes in many tongues. From somewhere below came the noise of glassware breaking and, from the city, a smell of burning. The taste and stench and sound of defeat—a defeat so swift and treacherous that she could still scarcely credit what had happened.

She looked bleakly at the towering figure of the cyborg. The creature's presence sent a sick shiver through her body. She was filled with anger, dismay, and revulsion as she thought: *I subsidized this thing. I created this madness.*

She gathered herself and stood proudly. She still wore the Imperial scarlet, and she was a Vykan queen. "Why have you done this thing?" she demanded.

The cyborg's eyes were cold, inhuman. "At least you don't tax me with treachery," Tallan said. "That would have been ironic, indeed."

"I tax you with nothing, cyb," Marlana spat out the epithet. "Irony is a *human* prerogative."

The cyborg stood with uncanny stillness. It seemed to Marlana that not a muscle in that great frame moved. "Kelber programmed me well, after all," he said. "In four thousand years men have still not learned. But that does not matter. Your city is my city now. And wasn't it great Glamiss who said: 'Who rules Nyor rules the stars?'"

Marlana felt the stomach-wrenching fury of a royal rage. "You took my city because we thought you came in my service, cyb. But can you hold it?" She could hear her voice rising, growing shrill with the force of her disgust and bitterness. "Will the star kings follow a cyborg?"

Again that inhuman stillness. The Sarissan did not move. *Great Spirit*, Marlana thought wildly, *the thing does not even breathe*. Behind the expressionless eyes tiny sparks seemed to be moving, gleaming and fading like witchfires. *No*, she thought, *surely I imagine that. It is alive, after all. Truly alive. It could be killed.*

"No," Tallan said impassively, "the star kings would not follow a cyborg. I should have to meet each one in combat and kill him. Your human ways would demand it. That is why I have kept it from them." He turned slowly to regard the closed door—as though he could see through the wood, Marlana thought, shuddering. "Only three humans knew what I am, Queen. Kelber, Landro—and you."

Marlana's hand went to her throat involuntarily. "Kelber is dead."

"And Landro."

It was like a blow. Marlana felt a deep and chilling sense of loss. Her eyes filled with tears. It shocked her to know that it mattered so. That silly, sweet-scented man—that buffoon and tool of women. Landro, dead.

Then the import of what the cyborg was saying reached her, and she was truly afraid.

"There's no need," she said faintly. "I can help you—"

The cyborg said, "No."

She thought: *It comes now, then, that death I have brought to others—so many others.*

For a moment she thought she might fall, beg. But it would do no good. The thing was not a man.

Her pride returned. Vyks could be greedy and treacherous, vain and cruel, like all men. But they were proud—and royal Vyks proudest of all.

The cyborg stood before her like a pillar of doom. He seemed to block out the light.

A great crack of thunder rattled the mullioned windows. It rolled across the citadel like a wave out of the sky.

Tallan turned.

Beyond the gallery Marlana could hear cries of warning and shouted commands.

Tallan left her and stepped to the door. A Sarissan warman stood saluting. Others, in the gallery, were running by.

"Starship, Warleader. The Rhad."

Marlana felt a great, leaping hope. A reprieve. A day, an hour, *anything*. The Rebel and his troops had returned.

"How many?" Tallan asked.

"One ship, Warleader."

Marlana sagged hopelessly. One ship. The Rebel had come to join the rebellion, not to challenge it. She closed her eyes in despair.

Tallan said in that cold voice like the sound of a drum across a wintry field, "Your time is not yet, Marlana."

He closed the door behind him, and she was alone with her thoughts.

Aboard the Rhadan vessel, Kier was arming. He wore his finest ceremonial armor, and his cape and helmet were bright with the feathered badges of his rank.

Cavour said, "Reason with him, Ariane. At least let us make a foray in force. He cannot force the cyborg to fight him."

"But I can," Kier said.

Nevus, the general, stood frowning. "With a thousand Rhad at our backs—"

Kier regarded the old warrior with affection. "I share your faith in the fighting qualities of the Rhad, Nevus. But ten thousand men wouldn't suffice to take Nyor, and you know it."

Ariane stood torn between pride and grief. "If this is for me, Kier, I ask you not to do it. I *beg* you, Kier—"

Kier touched her soft cheek with a mailed hand. "It is not for you, Ariane. You know what it is for."

"The Empire," she said angrily, tearfully. "Let the Empire go, Kier."

"You do not mean that, Queen."

The girl's voice was low. "No, I do not mean it."

"I say again that you can't make a cyborg fight you, Kier," Cavour insisted.

"I said that I can."

"How, in the name of the Spirit? How can you? Why shouldn't he simply have you taken?"

Han the Vykan fastened the last buckles of Kier's mail. He belted him with a star king's ceremonial weapons: sword, barbed flail, and dagger.

Brother Yakob appeared breathless in the torch-lighted compartment.

"Starship grounding, Warleader."

Kier acknowledged the priest's message and commanded, "The Navigators stay aboard."

"Yes, King."

"And tell Gret that it is time."

"I shall, Warleader."

Kier said to Cavour, "Tallan doesn't know it, Warlock, but he must fight me. He cannot refuse and rule."

"Black space, *why?*" Cavour's face was bleak with despair.

"Honor."

The warlock threw his hands in the air. "What has honor to do with a cyborg? What does Tallan know of *honor?*"

"It's a human concept," Kier said wryly. "And if he would wear Imperial scarlet, he must learn of it."

"Impossible. Insane."

"No," Nevus said roughly. "Kier is right on that point. If he challenges, Tallan must fight or be discredited before the star kings."

Ariane studied Kier's metal-masked face. She understood, as Nevus did. In a feudal society, loyalties stood or fell with the concept of *honor*.

But a cyborg, she thought fearfully, was a demon.

The enlightened part of her mind rebelled at the idea, but there it was, lurking deep among the superstitions of a lifetime.

She said, low, to Cavour, "If he fights the cyb— can he win?" She would have said "can he live," but the thought of Kier dead was too dismaying to put into words.

Cavour shook his head. "I think not, Queen."

Ariane turned away and made the sign of the Star. Inaudibly, she breathed her prayer. "Beatified Emeric protect him." All the stars in the galaxy would be meaningless to her without her rebel.

The Rhadan party left the starship with all the pomp and ceremony their limited numbers would allow.

Kier, flanked by Nevus and Ariane in Rhadan war harness and followed by a mixed guard of Vyks and Rhad, guided his nervous war mare through a landing ground crowded with starships from half a dozen systems across the galaxy.

At the rear of the small column rode the Vulks, eyeless and silent. The gathered warmen regarded them with suspicion, and many made the sign of the Star to ward off spirits.

Each starship, Kier noted, was carefully guarded by a war band of its own nationality. He studied the defenses and said to Ariane, "You see, it begins already. We have the makings of a fine little war right here."

Ariane, her face hidden behind the metal mask of her Rhad helmet, gentled her fractious mare with a thought and nodded. She did not trust herself to speak. Her eyes searched the hostile eyes of warmen from the rebellious worlds and saw that the Lyri hated the Betelgui, the Altairi the Denebians; the Sarissans hated them all. It was this suspicion and mistrust that the

Empire had held in check.

At the Nyor gate, the Rhad party was met by a party of heavily armed soldiers from Altair. "We are to take you to the warleader," the officer said brusquely.

Nevus rode forward and spoke in his harshest parade ground tones. "This is Kier, the star king of Rhada, warman. Don't they teach military courtesy in Altair?"

The Altairi stared at the old general for a moment, but he could not hold the gaze of those deep-set, commanding eyes that had seen a hundred battles before he, the Altairi, lifted his first sword.

"Apologies, general," he muttered sullenly. He turned to his men and ordered, "Honors for the star king, warmen."

The detachment lifted their weapons in salute and fell in on the flanks of the Rhadan troop.

Cavour, riding abreast of Han the Vykan, murmured, "It seems to me that we have done all this before."

Han said, looking admiringly at the riders at the head of the column, "See how bravely she rides, Warlock. She's not afraid."

The warlock studied the youngster's face and asked, "Are you?"

"Yes," Han replied in a quiet voice. "What will happen now?"

"Kier will challenge Tallan to the traditional Three Encounters."

"And then?"

The warlock did not reply. He shook his head and rode on in silence.

In the great hall of the citadel of Nyor, the rebel star kings and their higher officers had hastily gathered to see Kier of Rhada accept the overlordship of Tallan of Sarissa as warleader.

When Tallan entered, the warmen clashed their swords against their armor in applause. The Sarissan had led them to greater booty than they had imagined possible. Those few who still remembered their pledges to Glamiss and his son remained silent and thoughtful.

There was a smell of burning in the air. From the heights of the citadel could be seen the rising smoke from districts put to the torch by rampaging parties of off-world warriors. The ancient piers along the East River were charred ruins, and the estates of the wealthy clustered at the north end of Tel-Manhat were being looted and burned.

Isolated bands of Vegans, betrayers betrayed in their turn, were fighting desperate holding actions in the streets, and streams of Nyori refugees were gathering on the western banks of the island, trying to reach the imagined safety of the Jersey shore and the camp of the Vyks.

Tallan took his place at the head of the long chamber as the Rhadan delegation appeared.

Kier, standing in ceremonial war gear at the foot of the hall, studied the cyborg. His heart was thudding under his armor, and he felt weighed down by the weight of his weapons, but his face, half hidden by the mask of his helmet, remained impassive.

Ariane, seeing the cyb for the first time, felt her breath catch. Kier was tall among men of his time and strongly muscled. But the Sarissan was enormous—two full handspans higher than the Rhad. To Ariane, his mailed arms looked like tree trunks, the breadth of his chest and shoulders gigantic.

Erit touched her hand and whispered, "Courage, Queen."

Cavour measured the cyborg with a scientist's eye and came to the same dread conclusion that was dismaying Ariane. No human being could fight such a creature and live.

The star king of Deneb, a squat, scarred man who had fought beside Kier at the Battle of Karma, stepped forward and made a conciliating gesture. "You are late, cousin of Rhada. But better late than not at all. Welcome to our new order."

Kier walked deliberately forward, his eyes cold under the brow of the helmet. He said evenly, "I do not know you, warman."

The battered face of the Denebian king darkened, but before he could speak again, Kier had walked on to face Tallan.

The cyborg stood with that same stillness that had so disturbed Landro and Marlana. The hooded eyes alone seemed touched with strange life.

Kier said, "I have not come to join you, cyb. I have come to kill you."

A low growl of anger swept the room.

Tallan said, "I know."

"I called you cyb." Kier's voice was ringingly clear. There were cries of "Liar!" and worse among the ranks of the kings. These hard-bitten fighting men would never be convinced that they had followed an android—a creature so legendary that only a few warlocks believed it could exist other than as an evil spirit. Here and there an older warman made the sign of the Star. A cyborg might be a myth, but a demon could be something else again.

Kier drew back a gauntleted hand and struck Tallan across the face—three ritual blows. For a moment the cyborg's flesh flamed and then quickly paled. Cavour, his warlock's mind racing, concluded that this was not the effect of anger but of a superior body responding to attack with precision and economy.

Would a cyborg have the circulatory system of a man? Probably not. If a true scientist were to design a human being, he would be more efficient—produce a body that was not only stronger but also more resistant to injury. Cavour reckoned with sinking heart that a cyborg could not be weakened by ordinary wounds. The thrusts would have to be swift—and mortal.

The chamber was in an uproar. Kier had struck the three ritual blows of challenge. There could be no reply but combat to the death.

"Where shall it be?" the cyborg asked.

Swords clashed excitedly against armor.

Kier dropped his feathered cape and stood with his hands on his weapons.

"Here. And now," he said.

Chapter Seventeen

The Three Encounters was a form of personal combat reserved to individuals of kingly rank. The challenge was ritually delivered by three blows, and the response was customarily an instant commitment to battle. The form of the battle was established during the early years of the Interregnum and consisted of three stanzas of combat fought with the ceremonial weapons of kingship: the sword, the flail and the dagger. The first two encounters were limited in time to five minutes with a two-minute period for rest and assistance after each. Historians suggest that this peculiarly formalized form of combat derived from the ancient pugilistic battles of the Dawn Age, but this is conjecture. The third, and final, encounter was fought with the dagger and was to the death. Of course, a combatant could be killed at any stage of the fight, and frequently was.

Nv. Julianus Mullerium,
Ritual Combat in the Age of the Star Kings,
middle Second Stellar Empire period

KIER'S first warning of the assault was a roar from the assembled warriors.

His sword had only just cleared the scabbard before he saw the cyborg's blade descending with a shocking accuracy and swiftness. He caught the blow on the flat of his own sword and felt the stunning force of it run through his arm and body.

In the next instant, he was fighting for his life.

The cyborg fought with a cold dispassion and efficiency that would, in other circumstances, have filled Kier with admiration. It was as though a superior master-at-arms were conducting a class in the precise use of weapons. Each move was exactly as a hundred years and more of fencing masters had written it. Thrust, parry, and riposte followed in a classic, perfectly executed sequence. But each move was backed by a force and agility Kier had not imagined possible.

Within moments, the Rhad was drenched with sweat and aching with the impact of blow on blow that set god-metal ringing.

Tallan, fighting without a helmet, seemed to loom before him like a monstrous wall of spiked force. Each attack Kier was able to launch was met by a parrying blade and followed instantly by counterattacks delivered in textbook fashion.

Kier could hear the star kings shouting savagely, and he felt the rasp of breath in his throat. He dared not take his eyes from Tallan for the space of an instant.

The clangor of blades filled the room, and gradually Kier became aware that the metallic noise of battle was all that he could hear.

Tallan seemed to sense his growing fatigue, and his attack increased in vigor. Kier could not have said that it increased in fury, for there was a coldness to the battle that was unlike anything he had ever encountered in war.

As the combatants moved about the hall, the crowd of onlookers fell away, and the bloodthirsty shouts died until there seemed to be no one in the hall but the cyborg before Kier.

Kier could feel himself tiring. Each blow caught on his sword seemed to smash through his body like the impact of a battering ram. The cyborg's calm eyes fixed him, measured him. He felt himself being steadily forced backward, step by step.

Suddenly, there was a ripping pain across his side. He had seen the thrust coming and had not had the strength to parry it completely. *Now,* he thought, as the blood ran hot under his pierced mail shirt, *he'll finish me*. There was no despair or fear, for the euphoria of battle was upon him, and he had become exalted with the strange mixture of fatalism and joy that filled the Rhad when they did combat.

But the cyborg fought on as before: coldly, methodically. The style and force combined to produce a virtuoso performance with the sword, but there was not the hot drive of human savagery. Kier felt a tingle of desperate hope.

"Enough!" The squat Denebian had stepped between the combatants, signaling the end of the first encounter.

Kier dropped his sword from his aching hand and stood, legs apart, sucking in breath. His side was numb and wet. He would have stumbled but for Cavour and Han the Vykan rushing to his side and guiding him into the ranks of the silent Rhadan party.

Kier could feel Cavour lifting his armor and calling

for bandages to stop the blood flowing down his ribs. Nevus said, "The creature is a devil."

Ariane, her eyes filled with mingled fear and relief, held onto his mailed hand. She asked Cavour, "Is the wound bad?"

"Bad enough," the warlock replied, working to bind it.

Kier looked at Erit and Gret. The Vulks were strangely silent, unmoving.

"The flail!" the Denebian called. "The encounter of the flail!"

The star kings rumbled. The first stanza of battle had disturbed them, and they could not say how. None had ever seen Tallan of Sarissa fight, and the strange coldness of the engagement troubled them.

Han shook free the chains of the barbed flail and handed the weapon to Kier. His young face was pale. "The Star be with you, Warleader," he said.

Kier's fingers closed over the grip of the cruel weapon, and he stepped forward. His side was beginning to stiffen, and he knew that he must press the attack with all his remaining strength or be defeated.

He snapped the chains forward in a low attack, aiming at the hem of Tallan's mailed shirt. The air hissed with the speed of the barbs, and Kier felt the tips strike home. The god-metal of the Sarissan's armor bent and ripped, and the barbs bit into the flesh underneath.

A trickle of pale blood flowed down the cyborg's thigh. Nothing more. Kier's hope faltered. The creature hardly bled. A man would have been crippled by such a blow.

The cyborg moved forward, and for a time Kier could only catch the whistling chains again and again on the haft of his own flail as he was once again forced backward steadily, step by step.

The legends of cybs and demons rose in the Rhad's mind, and he wondered desperately if this cruelly methodical fighting creature before him was not, actually, some devil risen from the dark dead.

His foot struck the base of a stone column, and he twisted to avoid a smashing blow. He could not. The stones beside him took the main force of the stroke, but there was still force enough in it as it caught his chest to drive the breath from him, rip his mailed shirt, and lay his flesh open to the ribs. He heard Ariane's despairing cry.

On one knee now, he parried a second downstroke with his flail, and the chains became entangled. Tallan snapped his flail away with a swift movement, and Kier drove himself to stand, desperate and unarmed, against the column.

Death seemed but an instant away in the heavy silence of the crowded chamber. Kier's body seemed on fire with the pain of his wounds, and he watched with stony eyes as Tallan raised his flail for the finishing blow.

"Enough!" Kier could scarcely believe that the second encounter was finished or that Tallan could stop the descending blow in time even if he wished.

But the blow did not fall. Tallan released his grip on the flail and turned away, as coldly as he had begun the combat.

Kier sagged against the column and closed his eyes. Ariane and Cavour were desperately at his side.

Cavour said, in a strangled voice, "King—you cannot win."

The fatalism of the Rhad, Kier thought ironically.

He fought against the blackness that flickered around the edge of his vision. It was as though inevitable death were stalking him.

He sank to the floor and rested against the column while Cavour worked feverishly on him.

Kier signaled the Denebian to him, and when the scarred face was near his, he said, "If I lose the next encounter, my people are to return to Rhada. They will not fight against you."

"That will not be enough for the Sarissan," the Denebian said.

"At least promise me that my aides will be sent home." Kier touched Han the Vykan's shoulder and Ariane's masked face. "The rest can stand hostage."

Ariane started to speak, but Kier pressed her shoulder with the last of his failing strength.

"That much I can promise, I think," the Denebian said somberly.

Kier closed his eyes and let his helmet fall to the flagstones.

He felt a warm presence.

Gret was at his side, Erit behind him. It seemed to Kier that Gret was speaking; yet the Vulk's thin lips did not move, and it seemed that time had slowed, almost stopped. The people around him, Ariane, Han, Cavour, Nevus—all seemed frozen, scarcely moving.

King—do not be afraid.

It was Gret. The mind-touch. Never before had Kier felt it so strongly. It had form and clear reality, a great, soothing warmth.

I could not do this alone. Erit is with us.

Kier nodded drowsily.

We can help you.

Yes, Kier thought.

We can do this, but there is danger.

Kier felt as though he were smiling. Danger, indeed. What greater danger could a man face than that fighting machine in human form that was destroying him bit by bit?

There are worse things than dying, King.

Gret, Erit. Gret-Erit. They were one. The thoughts came with luminous clarity now.

The danger is madness, King. An eternity of madness. We do not know what damage it would do to charge a human brain with Vulk powers.

There was no pain. There was only a timeless questioning. *Eternity?*

You once asked me if Vulks died, King. They die. All things die. But a Vulk lives for a human eternity. If we tamper with your mind and destroy it, you will live a Vulk lifetime, King.

How long? Kier asked, dreading the answer it seemed he already knew.

Twenty thousand years, King.

Twenty thousand years of madness. *Twenty— thousand—years!*

For a moment it seemed that all the demons of hell rose in Kier's mind: a sick and febrile revulsion, dark terror, winged furies from an eternity of horror.

He felt the sadness and the gentle grief of the Vulks.

He saw the stars, scattered like dust across the cosmos, and the Vulk loneliness, a billion years before men came to tell them that they were not alone in the universe.

The murders and the killings, the pogroms, the human fear—all these were as nothing to the Vulks because they shared creation with one other intelligent creature—man.

Come, he said.

• • •

"The Encounter of the Dagger!" the Denebian called.

Kier rose and stood. Ariane stared at him and felt a dread emptiness, a loss. The Vulks had touched him, only that. And now he stood, and his eyes were no longer the familiar Rhadan blue—they were dark and farseeing. She thrust her knuckles against her lips to stifle the sudden desperate fear that chilled her.

Kier stood quite still, his naked dagger in his hand.

He was aware of all the living beings around him. Ariane—a sadness there. Cavour—he could hear the thoughts of a man hungry for knowledge and buried in the dark confusions of a medieval mind. Nevus—thoughts of war there, bloody thoughts of battle. But even the battle plans were primitive, rough-hewn as the man himself.

He knew the turbulent minds of the star kings: greedy, savage—some fearful, some brave, some troubled. And beyond the confines of the hall he could sense the life of animals, of insects stirring in the jacaranda trees in the ravaged gardens, of gulls sweeping over the gray waters of the rivers.

He touched minds briefly with Gret-Erit and felt their warmth and comfort.

Tallan stood before him, in a fighting stance, knife extended. Kier realized that he could read the cyborg as Gret could read ancient machines. Within the cyborg's skull Kier could sense the flashing circuitry of the ancient artifact that gave the creature life.

Pseudo-life.

Even that, like a Vulk, Kier was reluctant to destroy.

Tallan swept forward, and Kier felt the surge of subconscious terror in the onlookers that was the source of the cyborg's power over these primitive men.

Unwillingly, Kier drew his weapon back. In the electronic brain of his adversary was something like hate, but it was not hate.

It was the purpose of a machine—built by men to destroy men.

Kier's arm moved with inhuman swiftness. His blade flashed across the intervening distance and buried itself in the cyborg's skull.

Kier could see the wild sparking of severed circuits flashing with a kind of desperate vitality—

—into a kind of death.

The cyborg stiffened. His limbs jerked in a spasmodic, toylike dance. Then he crashed to the floor, a ruined colossus.

Kier felt the awed fear of the star kings, then their terror as they realized that they stood hostages now for the failure of the rebellion.

Gret-Erit-Kier agreed: *It is best that they do not know. Any of this.*

Kier said, "Let him be buried as a star king. It is his due."

He felt a great, sad regret. The wonder of man, he thought, that he could create such an instrument—a thing the non-mechanical Vulks could never have done—but to such ignominious purpose.

The star kings were clashing their weapons.

Kier felt Ariane behind him. He turned and looked on her with Vulk eyes: loving, ancient, tender with the affection of a father for a small child.

He took the helmet from her head, and the star kings stared at the daughter of Glamiss.

Someone murmured, "Queen-Empress—!"

Kier shook his head. "Han," he said quietly. "Go into the Galacton's chambers. You will find Marlana there. She will take you into the tel. Go with her and bring the Galacton here."

Ariane stared fearfully at Kier, so strangely possessed.

Within minutes, Han had returned. With him were Marlana and a grimy Torquas, rubbing at his eyes and staring at the assembled kings.

Ariane said, "How did you know, Kier?"

"I knew."

"I am the Galacton," Torquas announced petulantly.

The star kings, moving like a silent wave, knelt.

Torquas turned to regard his wife frowningly. "You had me locked away, Marlana. I could have you killed."

Marlana looked haggard and old. "I beg for mercy, husband," she said. Kier could sense the fear and the mingled hope for fresh plots in the woman's mind.

He intervened.

Torquas declared, "You are not my wife any longer. You are divorced. You will return to Vyka and stay there."

Marlana bowed her head.

Torquas said clearly, "Ariane is regent."

The star kings clashed their weapons again. And Kier turned away from the arguing and quarreling that began almost at the instant that they knew their lives were, for the moment at least, safe. Vykans from across the river were pouring into the city to restore some order. Kier felt a great weariness. He saw Ariane as though from an immense distance. Strange images of winged things and colored beams of light filled his thoughts.

The creature Gret-Erit-Kier was disintegrating. He understood this and knew what the price might be.

Will it be madness, then? he asked.

Gret-Erit replied, *We do not know, brother.*

Kier turned and walked away, wanting to be under the sky when it came.

It was growing dark.

Here and there, in the deepening darkness of the sky, Kier could see a star. For a long while he stood alone listening to the sounds around him, sensing the flow of life. It seemed to him that the power to know was fading away, leaving only strange images.

A man leading a ragged army with strange weapons across a snowy wasteland. He could not tell how he knew it, but that was an image of the past.

Three gaunt figures on crosses atop a hill that in the muttering dusk looked like a skull—

A sweeping vision of star clusters and suns without number, the center of the galaxy seen as only a Navigator might see it from the bridge of a great starship—

Hallucinations? The beginnings of an eternity of grief and terror? Or the accumulated memories of a race old before man was born?

The images faded and with them the sense of sharing the life of all things under the sky.

The power was going. The human mind was not yet ready to accept it. Kier felt a deep and gentle sadness.

He heard a voice behind him. It was Ariane. And he had *heard* her, not sensed her.

She came to him and looked into his troubled, shadowed eyes. She saw the sadness, but they were once again the eyes of a man.

"Will you tell me one day, Rebel?" she asked gently.

Kier slipped his arm about her and looked again at the sky. The stars were much brighter, and from

horizon to horizon stretched the edge of the galactic
lens that men, time out of mind, had called the Milky
Way.

"One day, Ariane, I will tell you," he said. "If I
can."

Across the deepening night a meteor flashed with
brief intensity. It seemed to Kier that it was like the
life of a man against the night of history. And if it
seemed brief and to no purpose, at least it burned
brightly and gave a touch of light to the dark.